Keith stared at the photos of himself when he was Scott's age.

He thought of the woman's comments. She had been right. Scott looked *exactly* the way Keith had looked when he was young. Same shape face, same body type, same stance, same smile and the same eyes.

Callahan eyes.

I would have known him anywhere.

Keith could hardly breathe. His mind counted backward. December to November. November to October…

He had been in Austin then. *This must be my son. He looks exactly like me....*

Dear Reader,

Back by popular demand, MONTANA MAVERICKS: RETURN TO WHITEHORN reappears in Special Edition! Just in time for the Yuletide season, unwrap our exciting 2-in-1 *A Montana Mavericks Christmas* collection by Susan Mallery and Karen Hughes. And next month, look for more passion beneath the big blue Whitehorn sky with *A Family Homecoming* by Laurie Paige.

Reader favorite Arlene James makes a special delivery with *Baby Boy Blessed*. In this heartwarming THAT'S MY BABY! story, a cooing infant on the doorstep just might turn two virtual strangers into lifelong partners…in love!

The holiday cheer continues with *Wyoming Wildcat* by Myrna Temte. Don't miss book four of the HEARTS OF WYOMING series, which features a fun-loving rodeo champ who sets out to win the wary heart of one love-shy single mom. And you better watch out, 'cause *Daddy Claus* is coming to town! In this tender tale by Robin Lee Hatcher, a pretend couple discovers how nice it might be to be a family forever.

Rounding off a month of sparkling romance, *Wedding Bells and Mistletoe* by veteran author Trisha Alexander launches the CALLAHANS & KIN miniseries with a deeply emotional story about a forbidden passion—and a long-buried secret— that can no longer be denied. And dreams come true for two tempestuous lovers in *A Child for Christmas* by Allison Leigh— the next installment in the MEN OF THE DOUBLE-C RANCH series.

I hope you enjoy all these romances. All of us here at Silhouette wish you a joyous holiday season!

Best,

Karen Taylor Richman,
Senior Editor

Please address questions and book requests to:
Silhouette Reader Service
U.S.: 3010 Walden Ave., P.O. Box 1325, Buffalo, NY 14269
Canadian: P.O. Box 609, Fort Erie, Ont. L2A 5X3

TRISHA ALEXANDER

WEDDING BELLS AND MISTLETOE

Silhouette®

SPECIAL EDITION®

Published by Silhouette Books

America's Publisher of Contemporary Romance

SILHOUETTE BOOKS

ISBN 0-373-24289-1

WEDDING BELLS AND MISTLETOE

Visit us at www.romance.net

Printed in U.S.A.

Books by Trisha Alexander

Silhouette Special Edition

Cinderella Girl #640
When Somebody Loves You #748
When Somebody Needs You #784
Mother of the Groom #801
When Somebody Wants You #822
Here Comes the Groom #845
Say You Love Me #875
What Will the Children Think? #906
Let's Make It Legal #924
The Real Elizabeth Hollister... #940
The Girl Next Door #965
This Child Is Mine #989
*A Bride for Luke #1024
*A Bride for John #1047
*A Baby for Rebecca #1070
Stop the Wedding! #1097
Substitute Bride #1115
With This Wedding Ring #1169
A Mother for Jeffrey #1211
†*Wedding Bells and Mistletoe* #1289

*Three Brides and a Baby
†Callahans & Kin

TRISHA ALEXANDER

has had a lifelong love affair with books and has always
wanted to be a writer. She also loves cats, movies, the
ocean, music, Broadway shows, cooking, traveling,
being with her family and friends, Cajun food, "Calvin
and Hobbes" and getting mail. Trisha and her husband
have three grown children, three adorable grandchildren
and live in Houston, Texas. Trisha loves to hear from
readers. You can write to her at P.O. Box 441603,
Houston, TX 77244-1603.

The Callahan Family Tree

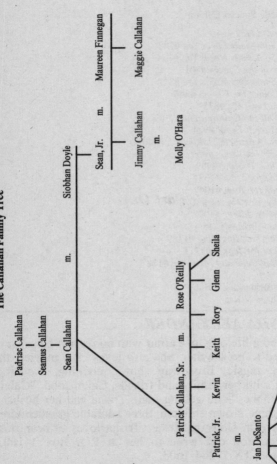

Part One

Chapter One

"I can't wait for you to meet Susan."

Keith Callahan rolled his eyes at Paul Sheridan, his best friend. "I know, I know, she's wonderful, she's perfect, she's awesome and you're nuts about her."

Paul's expression became sheepish. "Yeah. She *is* pretty special."

"So when *am* I going to meet her?"

"Tonight."

Keith had arrived in Austin the previous evening. It was Paul's spring break—he was a senior at the University of Texas—and he normally would have spent the time off at home in Rainbow's End, where they'd both grown up. But Paul hadn't wanted to leave Susan, who couldn't afford to take time off work, so Keith had come to Austin instead.

Being there was no hardship for Keith. Rainbow's End was only ninety minutes west of Austin, but the towns could have been in separate universes. Although Austin wasn't mammoth like Dallas or Houston, it was huge compared to Rainbow's End, whose total population was just under twelve thousand.

When Keith and Paul were young boys, they'd loved their hometown, but as they grew older, they'd felt stifled by its lack of excitement and opportunities for adventure. They'd spent many a long summer night fantasizing about leaving. They'd talked about how they would become forest rangers or wilderness guides somewhere like Wyoming or Alaska. Someplace exciting and different. The last place either wanted to end up was their boring hometown.

And yet it looked now as if that was where they would both spend the rest of their lives. Somehow, by high school graduation, Keith's family had pressured him into working in his family's construction business just like his two older brothers, and Paul had also succumbed to his father's wishes and would become a lawyer just like his father and grandfather before him.

Sometimes, though, Keith still entertained secret dreams of getting away. Now the dreams weren't centered around adventure so much as being free from the at-times smothering expectations of his family. And if it weren't for Paul, he probably would make the break. He wondered if Paul ever felt he might have made the wrong choice. Maybe this week they'd get a chance to talk about it.

It was a funny thing, Keith mused. He had four

brothers—two older and two younger—and they were a pretty close bunch, but Paul, who was not related by blood, was like his other half. Since kindergarten, they'd been inseparable. Keith remembered how his mother had always teased them, saying they must have been twins in another life.

"So what do you think?" Paul said now, breaking into Keith's thoughts. "How about this afternoon we go over to Tony's and shoot some pool?" He grinned. "Give me a chance to whup your ass."

Keith laughed. "In your dreams."

"Wanna put some money where your mouth is?"

"Ten bucks a game?"

"You got yourself a deal."

They spent a pleasant afternoon playing pool and drinking a couple of beers. Then it was time to get ready for their evening with Susan.

"Where does she live?" Keith asked when they started out.

"She has an apartment about fifteen minutes from here."

Keith frowned when Paul pulled his Bronco up before a small, run-down complex in an area that had seen better days.

"I know," Paul said, seeing Keith's expression. "It's kind of a dump, but Susan's putting herself through school, and money's tight."

"Her parents don't help at all?"

Paul shook his head. "Her dad skipped out on her mother when Susan was only two, and her mother barely made enough to keep a roof over their heads.

Then, when Susan was a senior in high school, her mother got cancer.''

"That's rough.''

"Yeah. Susan doesn't talk about it much, but she took care of her mother the whole time she was sick. She died a couple of years ago. That's why Susan's barely a sophomore now instead of a senior, like she should be.''

Keith couldn't imagine losing both his parents. Shoot, he couldn't imagine losing *one* of his parents. Anytime he'd ever thought about it, he had pushed the thoughts away, because it wasn't a place he wanted to go.

They walked across a cracked parking lot toward the apartments. Keith looked at the cars parked there—mostly old, inexpensive models. He studied the small complex. He couldn't help comparing it— with its badly-in-need-of-paint exterior—to the bright, new complex Paul lived in, complete with sparkling pool, tennis courts and maid service. Of course, Paul's digs were paid for by his mother, who doted on him, all the more so since his father had died unexpectedly the year before.

He looked at Paul. "So Susan was left with no money when her mother died?''

Paul shrugged. "She got a little bit. There was a small insurance policy, just enough to pay the medical bills with some left over, but as far as I can tell, that's mostly gone now. I've been trying to persuade her to move in with me.'' By now they'd entered the complex and were headed toward Susan's unit. "But she won't.''

"Oh, yeah?" In Keith's experience, most girls couldn't wait to move in with a guy. They usually viewed living together as the first step on the road to getting the coveted wedding ring. "She's holding out for marriage, huh?"

"Susan's not like that," Paul said stiffly. "She's got high principles. I admire that about her."

Keith was getting the feeling that Susan was just a little bit too good to be true. No one could be as perfect as Paul had painted her.

"This is her place." Paul walked up to a door marked with the number eighteen and rang the doorbell. A few moments later, the door opened.

The girl who stood there was nothing like Keith had pictured her. Paul usually went for tall blondes. Sexy, tall blondes with long legs. Susan Carroll was small, maybe five foot three, with curly, light brown, shoulder-length hair held away from her face by a white headband. Her big brown eyes looked straight at you. She was the kind of girl Keith's mother would describe as "cute," with freckles sprinkled across her nose and a girl-next-door look, which was accentuated by her outfit of jeans, white blouse and brown loafers.

"Hi," she said, smiling up at Paul, who was grinning at her like a fool.

"Hi," he said, bending down to kiss her. She had turned her head slightly, and the kiss landed on the corner of her mouth. For some reason, Keith got the feeling the movement had been intentional.

Paul introduced them, and Susan stuck out her right hand. Her handshake was firm, her eyes curious as she met Keith's gaze. "It's nice to meet you, Keith. Paul talks about you all the time."

She had a low, husky voice. Bedroom voice, Keith thought, then was immediately embarrassed, even though she couldn't know what he was thinking. "When he's with me, he talks about *you* all the time."

She laughed—a throaty chuckle that made Keith wish he could think of something else amusing to say.

"I'm not sure if that means he has good taste or bad taste."

"Good taste, I'd say," Keith said, realizing he really meant it.

"Hey, you can let her hand go anytime now," Paul said.

Keith blinked. He hadn't realized he was still holding her hand. "Sorry." Feeling sheepish, he dropped it.

Paul threw his arm around Susan's shoulders. "Ready?"

She nodded. "Uh-huh. Just as soon as I lock up. Callie's gone."

"Callie's her roommate," Paul explained. "I was hoping she'd stick around this week, 'cause I thought you'd like her, but she went home to Dallas."

"You *would* have liked her," Susan said. "Callie's gorgeous."

"Hey," Paul said, "I think *you're* gorgeous." The look on his face was beyond sappy.

Yep, he had it bad, Keith thought. Real bad. But to be fair, even though Susan wasn't beautiful, the way Paul seemed to think, Keith could see what her appeal was. She made you feel good when you looked at her.

Susan locked the door, and they headed toward the truck. Politely, Keith insisted Susan ride in the front with Paul. Being polite had its advantages, he decided once they were on their way. By sitting in the back, he could study her without being obvious about it. He was very curious about her. She was so different from the girls Paul had dated in the past. Maybe all the good things Paul had said about her were true, after all, and not just the exaggerations of a guy blinded by an infatuation. Still, Keith would reserve his final opinion until he'd spent more time with her. Appearances could be deceiving, he reminded himself, remembering his own infatuation a few years back with a girl who had turned out to be something other than what he'd imagined.

"So what do you think?" Paul said. "Want to get something to eat first, then go to Maggie Mae's?" Maggie Mae's was a popular club on Sixth Street where they always had good music.

"That's fine with me," Susan said.

"I can always eat," Keith said.

After a brief discussion about what they felt hungry for, they settled on a hamburger place. It was the kind of restaurant where you place your order at the counter, then get your drink and find your own table.

After they were seated and waiting for their food to be ready, Susan turned to Keith. "Has Paul told you how envious of you I am?"

"Me?" Keith said. "Why?"

"Because you come from such a big family," she said wistfully. "I always wanted brothers and sisters, and the idea of having five siblings...well, I just can't imagine it."

"Believe me," Keith said, "sometimes you wouldn't want to imagine it."

Paul chuckled. "Yeah. Like when they fought, which was most of the time."

"You can say that again," Keith agreed. "I used to get pounded on a lot." He laughed at Susan's horrified expression. "I'm exaggerating. They didn't really pound on me. But I did get picked on."

"They pounded on him," Paul said, "but he deserved it. He was a pest."

"We were *both* pests," Keith corrected him. "Paul and I were always tagging along after my older brothers. They hated it. They always tried to sneak out without us." Keith drank some of his tea. "But we all get along great now."

"That's really nice," Susan said. "Tell me about them."

"You don't really want to hear."

"Yes, I do. I told you. I'm envious. Who's the oldest?"

"Okay. You asked for it. The oldest is Patrick. Patrick Jr., only he hates being called Junior. When we were kids, our mother called him Two."

"Two?"

"Yeah, you know...the second Patrick in the family."

Susan laughed. "Oh, I love that. That's great."

There it was again, that laugh—sexy and contagious at the same time. It kind of gave him an odd feeling to hear it. Yeah, he could definitely see why Paul liked her so much.

"So how old is Patrick?" Susan asked.

"Twenty-eight. He's the only one of us who's married. In fact, he's got two kids already. Two little girls." He smiled thinking of them. Jana and Katie were so cute, they'd made Keith think that someday he might not mind having a kid of his own.

"And after Patrick?" Susan prompted.

"Then comes Kevin," Paul said. "He's twenty-six. Right, Keith?"

"Right. And after Kevin comes me." He grinned. "I'm twenty-one, almost twenty-two."

"That's right," Paul said. "Your birthday is next month."

"Yep. April 15th. Tax day."

"Really?" Susan said. "My birthday is April 16th."

"It is?" Paul said. "You didn't tell me."

She shrugged. "Birthdays have never been a big deal in my family."

Her tone was nonchalant, but there was something—some spark of emotion in her eyes—that told Keith she wasn't as indifferent as she was trying to pretend. No, there was hurt there, he decided. And seeing it made him feel bad. He remembered how his mother had made a big production of their birthdays. Rose Callahan always said your birthday was the most special day of the year, because it belonged to you and no one else. In Keith's family, for the entire day of your birthday, you felt like the most important person in the world. It had been a great feeling.

Paul started to say something else about Susan's birthday, but she cut him off. Turning to Keith, she said, "We're getting off the track. So after you comes who?"

"After me comes Rory," Keith said, going along with Susan. If talking about what she'd missed made her feel bad, he wouldn't add to her discomfort. "He's nineteen. Then Glenn, who's sixteen. And last but not least is Sheila. She's thirteen and the baby, but boy, does she ever hate it when you call her that."

Paul laughed. "Yeah, she hauled off and punched me once when I called her 'the baby.' She's got a mean right hook."

Keith rolled his eyes. "That's our Sheila. Act first, think later."

Susan smiled. "They sound wonderful."

Keith nodded. "I make cracks about them all the time, but the truth is, they're a good bunch."

Just then, their number was called. "I'll go get the food," Paul said. "You two stay here and talk."

"Paul tells me your parents are terrific, too," Susan said after Paul left.

"Yeah, they are. My dad, he's tough. He doesn't stand for any guff from us kids, but he's fair. If he gets on us for something, we usually deserve it. And my mom...my mom, she's the greatest." At this last, he ducked his head a little, embarrassed by the sudden welling of emotion he felt talking about his family.

"You're so lucky," Susan said softly.

He looked up, and their eyes met across the table. In hers, he saw the glint of tears, and he knew she was thinking about her own mother. Something constricted in his chest. And in that moment, Keith knew Paul hadn't exaggerated. Susan was everything he'd said she was—a sweet, sensitive, just-plain-nice girl. Keith liked her. He liked her a lot. In fact, he found himself wishing he'd met her first. Paul was a very lucky guy.

That opinion was reinforced as the evening wore on. Even so, one thing about Susan bothered Keith. He wasn't sure she returned Paul's feelings. You could tell she liked him, but anytime he got sappy around her, she seemed uncomfortable. One time, toward the end of evening, Paul leaned over and tried to nuzzle her ear. She didn't make a big deal of it, yet she moved out of his reach. Her behavior puzzled Keith. If she wasn't in love with Paul, why was she stringing him along?

With another girl Keith might have thought she recognized a good thing when she saw it, and in love or not, she'd decided Paul was a good catch. After all, it was obvious Paul had money. The apartment he lived in, the new Bronco he drove, the nice clothes he wore, the abundance of spending money he had, and the fact that he didn't work all attested to the fact that his family was, if not wealthy, very comfortable. To a girl like Susan, who had so little, Paul would seem to have so much.

Yet instinctively Keith felt money wasn't important to Susan. At least not important enough to compromise her principles. Because Paul was right about that, too. Susan did have high principles. That was obvious in everything she'd said the entire evening.

So what was going on?

Later, after they'd taken Susan home and were back in Paul's apartment, Keith tried to think of a diplomatic way to introduce the subject of Susan's seeming lack of ardor toward Paul, when Paul made it easy for him.

"So what did you think?" Paul asked. "Isn't Susan great?"

"I liked her a lot."

Paul smiled happily. "I knew you would."

"So what's the story between you two?" Keith asked casually.

"What do you mean?"

"You know. You serious about her?"

He nodded. "I've asked her to marry me."

It surprised Keith to feel a stab of jealousy. "That's great," he said quickly. "You told your mother yet?"

Paul shook his head. "No. Susan said she isn't sure."

"What do you mean? Not sure about what?"

"It's no big deal. She's just cautious, that's all. But I'm not worried," he added confidently. "She just needs some time to get used to the idea."

Paul's answer didn't reassure Keith. Paul had a tendency to see only what he wanted to see. He'd always been that way.

That night, lying awake on the sofa, Keith thought about the evening. He wondered if Susan and Paul were sleeping together. Somehow, he didn't think so. When two people were having sex, they gave off vibes. And Keith hadn't sensed any of those vibes tonight.

No matter what Paul said, Keith was concerned his buddy was going to get hurt. The next morning, he almost said something, then thought better of it. He and Paul might be best friends, but there were some things friends didn't say. This was one of them. Paul's love life was his business and no one else's.

Besides, Keith might be imagining problems where none existed. Maybe Susan *was* just cautious, the way Paul had said. After all, Keith had only spent one evening with her, whereas Paul had been seeing her for months.

That was probably it, he thought with relief, and pushed the last, lingering doubts out of his mind.

Chapter Two

The next morning Keith woke up to the smell of frying bacon. He pulled on his jeans, then headed out to the kitchen. Paul was standing at the stove and turned around when Keith walked in.

"Two eggs or three?" he said, pointing to the open carton on the counter.

"Two." Keith poured himself a cup of coffee, then walked around and sat at the bar that separated the living room from the kitchen.

While Paul cooked, they talked about the Rockets' current season. They'd both played basketball in high school and still loved the game. When Paul was finished making their breakfast, he handed Keith their plates, then joined him at the bar. For a while, they ate in silence. Then Keith, remembering his thoughts of the day before, said, "Do you ever think about how we always wanted to leave Rainbow's End?"

Paul smiled. "And become forest rangers or wilderness guides?"

"Yeah."

"Sure, sometimes."

After a moment of reflection, Keith said, "I think about it a lot."

"I thought you liked working for your dad."

"Yeah, well, it's okay. But I don't know. Lately I've been thinking how much I'd like to get away from everything."

"From your family, you mean?"

"Just…everything. Don't you ever feel that way? Like you'd like to strike out on your own, not worry about what anyone else wants." Keith knew Paul's mother had become pretty possessive since his dad died.

Paul wiped his mouth on his napkin, then swiveled around to face Keith. "I used to feel that way, but not anymore. Not since I met Susan." Seeing Keith's frown, he smiled. "The thing is, I want to give her a good life. The kind of life where she feels secure. And I can't do that if I go off looking for excitement and adventure. That's the kind of thing you dream about when you're a kid, but it's not the kind of thing you do when you want to marry someone and have a family."

Keith felt half annoyed and half envious. "So you think I'm being childish because I still want to do something more adventurous than working construction?"

"No, I'm just saying you'll feel different when you meet somebody and fall in love."

Keith nodded reluctantly. Paul was probably right. If Keith had a girl like Susan, he'd probably feel exactly the same way Paul did. Trouble was, he didn't, and living in Rainbow's End, where Keith knew just about every female in or near his age group, it wasn't likely he'd meet anyone like her, either.

"Speaking of Susan," Paul said, "I thought today we could go have lunch at the restaurant where she works. That okay with you?"

"Sure." Keith had hoped he'd have another opportunity to observe Paul and Susan together.

For the rest of the morning, they hung out at Paul's place. Paul said it would be best to go to the restaurant after the main lunch crowd was finished, otherwise, Susan would be so busy she wouldn't have any time to talk to them.

She was obviously surprised to see them when they walked into the restaurant a little after one. "Hi! I didn't know you were coming today."

"I wanted Keith to see where you worked," Paul said.

Her eyes met Keith's. "Paul thinks everyone is interested in everything about me."

"Not everyone," he said. "Just Keith."

"I *am* interested," Keith said.

"Just don't get *too* interested," Paul countered, grinning at him. "She's mine."

"Paul!" Susan's cheeks were pink with embarrassment and she couldn't look at Keith. Her reaction caused Keith to feel oddly embarrassed, too, and instead of the snappy comeback he would normally have given Paul, he fell into an awkward silence. But Paul seemed oblivious and led the way to a booth.

By the time they were seated and had given Susan their order, she had recovered her equanimity, and so had Keith. They had a pleasant lunch, and Keith enjoyed watching her work. She was fast and efficient and obviously had a good relationship with the rest of the wait staff. Customers liked her, too, if the smiles they gave her were any indication, and Keith was sure they were. The thing about her, he decided, was that she gave off warm, friendly vibes, without being flirtatious.

When they finished lunch and were leaving, Paul asked her if she wanted to go out with them that night.

"I can't," she said. "I told Sandi I'd take her shift."

"Susan," Paul protested. "Working a double is too much."

She shrugged. "It's not that bad. It's not like I do it all the time."

"Well, how about tomorrow?"

"We'll see," she said. "I'll call you when I get home."

She did go out with them the following evening, and during the rest of the week, they spent as much time with her as she had free. They went to a movie one night and they went out to dinner another night.

Keith found himself liking her more and more. He wondered what she thought of him. Several times during the week, when he turned her way, he'd caught her watching him. Quickly, she'd averted her gaze. She was probably just curious about him, he figured, the same way he was curious about her. After all, if she *did* marry Paul, they would see a lot of each other.

The thought produced mixed emotions. If Susan and Paul married, things would be different between Keith and Paul. They were bound to be. There'd be no more going out at night, no more weekend trips, no more of most of the things they had done together as single guys. When he voiced this thought, Paul just said, "Guess we'd better find someone for you, then!"

The night before Keith was due to leave for home, Susan was scheduled to work, but Paul talked her into trading with someone so the three of them could spend one last evening together. Unfortunately, that morning, Paul woke up with a sore throat, and by afternoon, it was obvious he was too sick to go anywhere.

"I'll call Susan and tell her," Keith said.

"No. There's no reason for you two to stay home just because I'm sick," Paul said.

"I'm not going without *you*," Keith insisted.

"Look, Susan took the night off. I don't want her to waste it."

"But—"

"C'mon, Keith. What's the big deal?"

"No big deal. I just think—"

"Hey, I want you to go, okay?"

Because Keith could see Paul wasn't going to take

no for an answer, he finally agreed, but he knew it wasn't a good idea because the thought of spending an evening alone with Susan had produced a strange mixture of uneasiness and excitement, two emotions he was reluctant to analyze.

But what choice had he had?

At seven, when he knocked at Susan's door, the excitement had all but wiped out the uneasiness, and he could no longer deny he was looking forward to spending the evening with her.

When she opened the door, he sucked in his breath at the sight of her. She looked fantastic in a short red dress that showed off sensational legs. Suddenly, Keith knew he'd been right to be uneasy earlier in the day, because what he was feeling at this moment was not the way he should be feeling about his best friend's girl.

"Wow," he said in a voice that didn't sound like his. "You look great."

"Thanks. You…you look nice, too." She sounded breathless, and she didn't quite meet his eye.

As they walked to Keith's car, an awkward silence fell between them.

"I'm sorry—"

"Paul said—"

They broke off at the same time.

"Sorry," Keith said. "What were you going to say?"

She smiled. "Just that I'm sorry Paul's sick."

"Yeah, I know. He said to tell you not to worry about him, though."

"Yes, but I know Paul. He won't call the doctor until he's practically dying."

Keith grinned. "True." He deepened his voice. "We big he-men don't need doctors."

Susan rolled her eyes.

The exchange lessened the tension Keith had been feeling. Even so, he was all too aware of Susan sitting next to him as they drove to the restaurant where they had dinner reservations.

By the time they were seated across the dinner table from each other, Keith knew he should have listened to his instincts—the ones that told him to stay home tonight—because what he was feeling for Susan was dangerous.

It was a mistake to have come. But he could still make it okay. He could pretend *he* wasn't feeling well, either. He could take Susan home and go back to Paul's as soon as dinner was over.

But even as he thought about doing it, the waiter came, and they ordered, and once he was gone, Keith felt dumb. He was overreacting. So he was attracted to Susan. So what? He'd been attracted to a lot of girls. That didn't mean he had to act on the attraction, did it?

He told himself to cool it. He could enjoy the evening and her company as long as he kept reminding himself that she belonged to Paul.

There was nothing to worry about. He was an adult, and he could control himself. Everything was going to be fine.

"You're awfully quiet tonight."

"Sorry," Keith said. They had just placed their

order, and he'd been lost in his thoughts. He tried to think of something to say, but his mind was blank.

"You know, Keith..." Susan straightened her silverware and avoided his eyes. "It wasn't necessary for you to take me out tonight. I know you're probably bored, and I wouldn't have minded staying home. In fact, when we finish dinner, why don't you take me back—"

"I'm not bored, and I'm not taking you home when we're through with dinner. We're going to Tallulah's just like we planned." Now that she'd given him an out, perversely, he didn't want one.

"Well, if you're sure..." She looked up, her eyes soft and warm.

"I'm sure." She had the prettiest eyes he'd ever seen. A guy could drown in those eyes.

She looked away first, and Keith gave himself a mental shake. What was wrong with him? He couldn't seem to keep his mind away from the dangerous place it kept wanting to go. It was as if Susan had cast some kind of spell on him, he thought angrily. But he wasn't angry with her. He was angry with himself.

Determinedly then, if only to prove he could, he kept a light, impersonal conversation going throughout dinner. But no matter what they were talking about, he was acutely aware of her. Of the way the candlelight played across her face and hair. Of the intoxicating fragrance of her perfume that kept drifting across the table and distracting him. Of her soft curves under the silky dress.

His eyes kept straying to the curve of her neck, to

the soft rise and fall of her breasts, to the fullness of her lower lip. He kept imagining what it would be like to touch her, to kiss her, to make love to her.

By the time dinner was over, he knew he was in trouble. Big trouble. He could no longer deny he wanted Susan. He wanted her more than he'd ever wanted anyone, and the more time he spent with her, the greater that wanting became. It was all he could do to keep the desire he felt out of his eyes and his voice. If he had any sense at all, he would summon up the guts to tell her that he hoped she wouldn't be disappointed, but he wanted to get an early start home tomorrow, so would she mind if they skipped the club, after all?

Say it, he told himself as he paid the check and they stood to leave. *Say it,* he told himself as they headed for the exit. *Say it,* he told himself as they walked out the door and down the front sidewalk toward the parking lot.

He actually opened his mouth, but just then Susan stumbled on the uneven concrete, and instinctively, Keith grabbed her to steady her. For a long moment, his hands remained at her waist. The desire that had smoldered all evening ignited into a blaze of longing.

She looked up, and he looked down.

"Susan," he whispered, his voice rough.

Afterwards, he didn't remember moving, but suddenly she was in his arms, and he was kissing her with a hunger that couldn't be denied. Once. Twice. Again and again. All rational thought disappeared. The only reality was Susan. Her mouth, so warm, so sweet, so impossible to resist. Her body, so pliant, so willing, so perfectly fitted to his.

It was only when they heard the sound of voices coming toward them that they finally pulled apart. Keith, dazed and shaken, didn't touch her as they walked unsteadily toward the car. He helped her in and, still feeling as if he were in a dream, walked around to the driver's side and climbed in himself.

For a few moments, they both sat there, silent. Then Keith cleared his throat. But before he could say anything, Susan said in a strained voice, "Please take me home."

"Susan..." Keith finally looked at her.

She stared straight ahead. "Please, Keith, don't say anything. J-just take me home."

He could tell she was fighting to maintain control of herself, and even though a dozen thoughts were flying around inside his head, and he knew he should apologize or *something,* he also knew if he said anything, she would probably break down. And then what would he do? He couldn't stand seeing a woman cry, especially if the crying had been brought on by something he'd done.

So he started the car, all the while cursing himself for being a jerk. A stupid, horny jerk. Why had he done it? What was wrong with him? Couldn't he keep himself under control for one night? To come on to her the way he had—that was inexcusable.

She wanted you, too.

Yeah, well, maybe she hadn't. Maybe he'd imagined she did because that's what he wanted to think. So he'd have an excuse for making a move on her.

She didn't resist you.

He glanced over at her. She sat rigidly, still staring straight ahead. Her profile looked as if it were carved in stone.

Suddenly, his anger at himself faded, and he was filled with a tenderness so profound, it was an ache in his chest. She looked so young and so vulnerable and so darned sweet sitting there.

His feelings confused him. Lust he understood. But this desire to hold her and comfort her, to tell her…what? His mind skittered away from the thought that kept trying to rear its head.

In silent misery, he drove her home.

As soon as Keith parked the car, Susan reached for the door handle. Her only thought was getting away from him, because if she didn't, she knew there would be a repeat of what had happened outside the restaurant.

Because she wanted him.

She'd wanted him from the first moment she'd laid eyes on him. Oh, she hadn't admitted it to herself, not immediately, anyway. And to be fair, maybe she hadn't even realized it, because the feelings she had for Keith were so foreign to her. He was the first man she'd ever felt this way about.

She still couldn't believe that she, Susan Carroll, the girl her high-school friends had called Miss Priss, because she was so proper and controlled and self-contained, had so completely lost sight of what was right and what was wrong that she'd given in to the feelings she knew would only cause her problems.

She clambered out of the car and, not looking at Keith, said, "You don't have to walk me to the door. I'm fine." She entered the parking lot and walked quickly toward her apartment.

"Susan, wait!"

She heard him coming up behind her. *Please, please. Go away. Please go away.* Her hands trembled as she fumbled in her purse for her keys.

"Susan," he said softly, laying his hand on her shoulder.

She bowed her head. Tears filled her eyes. *Please.*

Gently, he turned her to face him. She tried very hard to stop them, but she was too upset, and the tears overflowed.

"Ah, Susan, I'm sorry," he said.

Even then, she might have been able to resist him, if only she had pulled away. But the moment he put his arms around her, lowering his mouth to hers, she was lost.

They kissed for a long time. And then, silently, as if it were preordained and needed no discussion, he opened the door to her apartment, and they went inside.

They would make love, she knew. Tomorrow each might be sorry, but for now, being together like this was the only thing that mattered.

The moment the door closed behind them, they were in each other's arms. Impatient and hungry, they were filled with an urgency born of desperation and the unacknowledged awareness that if they went slower, they might have to think about what they were doing. They flung off their clothes, kissing each other and touching each other until they were in a frenzy of desire. Once begun, their lovemaking was like an avalanche, gaining speed and intensity until it was unstoppable. They wanted each other. Nothing else mattered.

For Keith, making love to Susan was unlike anything he'd ever experienced. It felt so incredibly right. Their bodies fitted together perfectly, as if they'd been made for each other. He plunged deep into her warmth, then deeper still. She gasped, wrapping her legs around him. His heart thundered in his chest as the shattering feelings built to an explosive release. Even as he was crying out, her own shuddering climax followed.

It was only afterwards, as Keith lay there holding Susan while their bodies cooled and their breathing slowed, that the reality of what they'd done hit him like a body blow.

Paul.

Keith felt sick.

Paul.

Who would go through fire for Keith. Who would lie down and die for Keith. Who was closer to Keith than his own brothers.

You've betrayed Paul. Done the worst thing, short of murder, any man can do to another.

But it *was* murder, wasn't it? Because if Paul knew what Keith had done, their friendship would be dead.

If Paul knew…

Keith couldn't even finish the thought. Couldn't

bear to think how Paul would feel if he were to ever find out about what had just happened.

As the full realization of what he'd done—and what the consequences of his actions might be—sank in, shame nearly overwhelmed him. Paul was lying in bed at home, sick and trusting Keith to take care of his girl. And Keith…Keith was lying in bed with said girl after having just had sex with her.

Suddenly, he couldn't stand being there another second. Pulling his arm out from under Susan, he got up. Not looking at her, he began searching for his clothes. Once he found them, he hurriedly started to dress.

"Keith?" There was uncertainty in her voice.

He fumbled with his pants and finally got them zipped, then shoved his feet into his loafers. Taking a deep breath, he turned to face her.

She was sitting up in bed. In the moonlight that spilled through her bedroom window, he could see that her face was stricken. In that moment, he felt lower than he'd ever felt. She didn't deserve what he was about to do, yet he knew he had no choice.

"Susan, I-I'm sorry. I have to go."

"But Keith, we—"

"I'm sorry," he repeated more desperately. "I-I hope you can forgive me."

He prayed she wouldn't cry. If she cried, he would never have the strength to leave her, and leave her he must. She was Paul's girl. What had happened between them tonight had been a terrible mistake, one he would spend the rest of his life regretting. And it must never happen again. That it *would* happen again if he stayed, there was no doubt in his mind. Although he was loath to examine his feelings for her too deeply, he knew that where she was concerned, he would never have the willpower to resist if she was within reach.

But she didn't cry.

And she didn't say a word.

She just sat there, watching him as he prepared to leave.

He almost changed his mind. More than anything, he wanted to walk back over to the bed, take her in his arms, and hold her there forever.

"I'm sorry," he said again.

And then he walked out.

The next hour was a blur. Trying to keep his mind blank, he drove back to Paul's apartment. Paul was sound asleep. Thank God, Keith thought. He couldn't have faced him.

As quietly as he could, Keith found some paper and a pen, and he wrote Paul a short note saying he had decided to get an early start for home and he hoped Paul was feeling better when he woke up.

Then Keith packed his duffel, climbed into his car and, with a heavy heart loaded with nearly unbearable guilt, headed home to Rainbow's End.

Part Two

Chapter Three

Ten years later

Almost home.

Keith's stomach tightened in anticipation as his beat-up Land Rover climbed the last hill before Rainbow's End would come into view. He wondered if he would find the town changed.

He sat forward, eager now for that first glimpse. And then there it was.

Rainbow's End.

Surprisingly moved, Keith pulled to the side of the road and stopped the truck. Climbing out, he walked to the crest of the hill and looked at the town below. It was spread across the valley in a neat mosaic, almost as if its design had been planned by far-seeing city fathers. Yet Keith knew the town had simply evolved, beginning with the home of his great-great-grandfather Padriac Callahan, who came to Texas in 1852 and planted the first Callahan roots.

Keith had heard the story many times. How Paddy's father Kealan and his mother Deirdre packed up their meager belongings and, along with Paddy and his younger sister Allene, left Ireland in 1847, a year after the great potato famine. Like most immigrants, they traveled steerage and landed in New York, where Kealan managed to find a place for them to live and enough work on the wharves to keep them all fed.

But the family was never happy in New York. Allene died of pneumonia a year after they arrived, and Deirdre, who was terribly homesick anyway, fell into a deep depression. Unable to make his wife happy and feeling like a failure, a despondent Kealan started drinking too much. One day on the job, suffering from a hangover, he was crushed by a falling crate.

By now Paddy was almost twenty years old, a big, strong lad who was fascinated by the lore of the western United States and most especially Texas, where, it was said, a young man who wasn't afraid of hard work could make his fortune. So with his mother in tow, Paddy headed west. He wasn't sure where he would settle, but figured he would know the place when he saw it.

Keith tried to imagine what his great-great-grandfather felt when he saw the view Keith was seeing now: the green valley surrounded by the low hills, the sparkling river winding its way across the valley floor that, in the spring, was covered with bluebonnets. The scene must have seemed like paradise after the tenements of New York and the long trek westward.

Family legend said it had been raining that day, a light mist that reminded Paddy and his mother of home, and that just as they crested the hill—the same hill Keith now stood upon—the sun broke through and crowned the valley with a glorious rainbow.

And so Rainbow's End had been born. And the Callahan family had lived there and thrived there for the past one hundred and forty-some years. Since Keith was one of six children, he imagined the family would continue to thrive for many more years to come. Although to hear his mother Rose tell it, if he and his slacker brothers and sister didn't hurry up and get married and give her a few more grandchildren, who knew how long the Callahans would last? Keith's older brother Patrick Jr. was the only one of the clan to marry so far, and unfortunately for the Callahan name, he and his wife Jan had only produced girls.

It wasn't for lack of trying, Keith thought affectionately. Still, after girl number four had been born six years ago, Patrick said they were throwing in the towel. "It's someone else's turn," he'd told Keith when he'd called to tell him about little Allene's birth.

"Don't look at me," Keith had said, laughing.

Eager now to see the family he'd been away from

for so long, Keith got back into the Rover, started it up again, and pointed it toward home.

Ten minutes later, he pulled into the driveway of the big brick Colonial his father had built for his new bride forty-two years earlier. He'd teased her for years, saying the main reason she married him was the fact that his family owned a construction company, and she knew she'd have a nice house, if nothing else.

Keith was relieved to see the house hadn't changed. The shutters on the red brick were still painted white, the front door still painted a shiny black. The azalea bushes planted on either side of the door were bigger, as was the oak tree in the side yard. Otherwise, the family homestead looked pretty much the same as it had the day Keith had left it to go to Alaska.

Just then the front door opened. Keith's heart contracted as he saw the familiar round shape of his mother outlined in the doorway. For a few seconds, she just stood there and he just sat there. Then, moving at almost the same instant, she hurried outside and he opened the door of the Rover and got out.

"Keith!"

"Mom!"

He caught her in his arms and, lifting her up, swung her around.

"Stop! Put me down!" she said, laughing. But her blue eyes, still bright, were filled with joy. "I'm so glad you're finally home," she said once he'd put her back on her feet. She patted his face the way she had when he was a little kid.

Looking at her, Keith's heart swelled with love. He nodded—he was too choked up to speak—and hugged her to him. An instant later, dozens of people poured out of the house and surrounded them. Hands pummeled him on the back, happy voices vied for attention, people laughed, as his entire family tried to greet him at once.

All his brothers were there, plus Patrick's wife Jan and their four girls. And his sister Sheila.

Keith was stunned when his eyes landed on Sheila. He'd seen pictures of her over the years he'd been away, but nothing had prepared him for how beautiful she was in the flesh. What a difference ten years had made. Like the rest of his siblings, she had very dark hair—almost black—but instead of having the bright blue Callahan eyes, hers were a soft shade of gray.

"They're just like my grandmother's," Rose Callahan always explained. "People said her eyes were the color of the Irish sky before a rainstorm."

"In other words," Keith's father always added, blue eyes twinkling, "the color of the Irish sky, period."

Sheila smiled up at Keith now.

"Hey, squirt," he said.

Her smile turned mischievous. "Hey, yourself."

He gathered her into his arms and kissed her cheek.

She hugged him tight. "I'm so glad you're home."

"Me, too."

"You old son of a gun," Rory said when Keith

had released Sheila. He threw his arms around Keith. "'Bout time you came home."

Keith hugged him back. Three years younger, Rory was his favorite brother.

"Yeah, Dad killed the fatted calf," added Patrick Jr. with just the slightest tinge of sarcasm.

"Which reminds me," Keith said, deciding to ignore the almost-implied criticism. "I'm starving." He had timed his arrival for Sunday afternoon dinner.

"Oh, good," his mother said, beaming. "So are the rest of this rowdy clan. But I wouldn't let them eat until you got here."

"Well, I'm here now."

Laughing and talking, they all trooped into the house.

"So what do you think?" his father said. "Is everything the way you remembered?"

"The living room looks different," Keith said. "Why did you buy new furniture?"

His mother laughed. "Keith. You've been gone ten years. Things wear out, you know."

He knew it was ridiculous to feel affronted, but somehow he had imagined the house would be exactly the way he'd left it.

"Don't worry," his mother added, "everything else is the same. Including your old room."

Entering the dining room, Keith could see she was right. The dark mahogany dining-room table was covered with the same lace cloth it had worn for more years than he could remember. Following his mother into the kitchen, he saw that the round maple kitchen table still had the grooves and scars left from dozens of hands, too. And the kitchen was still filled with the mouthwatering smells that had permeated the house throughout his growing-up years.

Keith lifted the lid of one of the pots on the stove. "Yesss! Mom's mashed potatoes." He stuck in a finger, then licked it. "Mmmmm. Even better than I remembered them, lumps and all."

His mother swatted at him with a pot holder. "My mashed potatoes do not have lumps! Now you get out of here. Go on in the dining room and sit down. The girls will help me serve."

Keith grinned at his sister and sister-in-law, Jan. "Okay, *girls,* get busy."

Sheila shook her fist at him, but she was laughing.

Keith walked back into the dining room and joined his brothers, who were milling around. He ruffled the heads of his nieces, looked at the family portraits adorning the walls and sideboard, and realized how much he had missed this.

"Son," his father said, clapping his hand on Keith's shoulder. "It's good to see you."

"You, too, Pop."

They smiled at each other. Keith was relieved to see his dad wasn't going to hold any grudges, although he also knew his father couldn't understand why Keith hadn't come home before this—at least for a visit.

And I can never explain it, Keith thought.

"Okay, now," his father said, "here comes the food. Let's all sit down."

It took a few minutes, but finally they were all seated around the big dining-room table, which prac-

tically groaned under the weight of all the food
Keith's mother had prepared. Keith's mouth watered
looking at it. There was boiled ham and cabbage,
mashed potatoes, broccoli with cheese, a marinated
salad, fried chicken, baked squash, and his mother's
big homemade yeast rolls—the ones he'd dreamed
about for years—dripping with butter.

Rory saw Keith's expression and grinned. "I'll bet
you haven't seen food like this since you left home."

"You're right."

"And whose fault is that?" Patrick Sr. said, but
the rebuke was a mild one and his expression held
affection instead of censure.

Once his mother and Sheila and Jan took their
seats, they all joined hands and Keith's father said
grace, ending with, "And thank you, Lord, for bringing home our beloved son, Keith. Amen."

"Amen," everyone echoed.

Keith swallowed against the lump in his throat, but
he wasn't allowed to feel sentimental for long. Soon
the conversation was flowing fast and furiously, the
way it always did with his family. Throughout dinner, Keith was peppered with questions. By the time
dessert—a wonderful-tasting, tart-apple pie—was
served, Keith figured there was only one question left
to ask. And finally, his mother asked it.

"How long are you going to stay?"

Silence fell around the table as everyone looked
Keith's way.

He shrugged. "I don't know."

"We were all hoping you were home for good,"
his father said.

"I know." He also knew they expected him to elaborate, but he couldn't. Because the reason behind his leaving Rainbow's End in the first place was not the one he'd given them. And even though some things had changed since then, Keith wasn't sure enough had changed. Suddenly, he knew he had to do something. Something that couldn't be put off. He pushed back his chair. "Listen, I'm sorry, but I have to leave for a while. I—I want to go out to the cemetery." He looked at his mother. "Do you mind, Mom?"

Her gentle face softened. "Of course not, honey. You go ahead. We'll all be here when you get back."

Murmurs of sympathy and assent came from the rest of the family members.

"You want company?" Rory said.

Keith shook his head. Although he would have liked to have Rory come along for moral support, he knew this visit was something he had to do alone.

Thirty minutes later, Keith stood in the still-hot, late-afternoon sunlight of the August day, and looked down at the well-tended grave site he'd had no trouble finding. The marble stone at the head of the grave was large and elegant and matched the one next to it, which belonged to Paul's father, Reginald Sheridan.

Keith's chest hurt as he looked at the words cut into this newer one:

Paul Reginald Sheridan
Beloved Son, Husband, and Father

Below were listed Paul's birthdate and the date of his death.

Keith fought back tears. Rory had written him eight months earlier to tell him about Paul's accident and death, and Keith had grieved then. But seeing Paul's grave made his death more real and Keith's feelings of loss and remorse more acute.

He had never gotten over his betrayal of Paul. That Paul didn't know about the betrayal didn't lessen Keith's feelings of guilt and self-disgust. The stark fact remained unchanged.

Paul. I'm so sorry. So very sorry.

After that night when Keith fled Austin, it didn't take him long to realize that there was no way he was going to be able to stay in Rainbow's End. How could he? To be that close to Paul and Susan every day of his life? Even if he could face Paul after what he'd done to him, Keith knew he could never be around Susan without remembering what they'd done. *Without wanting to do it again.* Just thinking about her caused him to feel that same stirring. That same longing. That same need.

In fact, it was all he could do to keep from calling her. Dozens of times, his hand had reached for the phone. And dozens of times, he'd pulled it back.

No, it would be impossible to stay in such close proximity. He couldn't trust himself around Susan. Sooner or later, he would give himself away. Worse, he might lose control and make a move on her again. The whole idea was unthinkable.

So a couple of weeks later, Keith told his father he had decided to do what he'd always dreamed of doing—go to Alaska. His family had tried to talk him out of it, but Keith wouldn't budge. And in April, one month after that fateful spring break, armed with his savings and his most prized possessions, Keith climbed into his car and made the long trek north.

He settled in the port town of Ketchikan for no other reason than he liked its rustic look and the friendliness of the natives.

He'd been lucky. He'd landed a job with an air-cargo company and eventually learned to fly one of the seaplanes they used to take supplies to outlying areas. It had been a simple life, but a good one. He'd worked hard, saved some money, made some friends, even had a girl for a couple of years. But he'd never fallen in love again. For by then, he had realized that was what had happened to him when he'd met Susan. Yes, he'd wanted her, but that was only the outward manifestation of what he'd felt. He'd fallen in love with her, and if he hadn't been so young and so appalled by the fact that Paul loved her, too, and wanted to marry her, he might have even done something about his feelings. Over the years he'd had plenty of time to think, and he'd wondered what would have happened if he'd stayed at Susan's that night. If they'd talked about things?

Instead, he'd run away, and the following fall Paul dropped out of law school and he and Susan married and had a son. They moved to Rainbow's End and Paul joined the sheriff's department.

Paul wasn't much of a letter-writer, but he did call Keith several times that first year, especially in the beginning. It was difficult talking to him. Keith tried to act as if nothing was wrong, but Paul had sensed something was different. And gradually, the phone calls stopped.

All those lost years, Keith thought now, his heart filled with regret. If only things could have been different. If only that night had ended differently. But it hadn't, and afterwards, Keith had done the only thing he could do at the time. He had distanced himself from Paul and Susan, hoping that with him gone, Susan might be able to forget and move on, maybe even build a life with Paul. And obviously, she had.

As he stared at the grave, he remembered the happy times. He hoped Paul had added to them these past years. That he and Susan had had a good marriage. That Susan wasn't haunted by the same guilt, the same memories, that had tormented Keith.

Susan.

Over the years, Keith had tried hard not to think about her. But today it didn't work. Images of her flooded his mind, followed by questions that had weighed on him ever since he'd heard about Paul's accident. How was she taking his death? Was she all right? What about their son? How was he handling the death of his father?

And then, even though he knew it was wrong, the other questions, the ones he'd tried never to voice, even in his thoughts, reared their heads. Did she ever think about that night? Did she ever think about him?

Suddenly, Keith knew he had been lying to himself for weeks, ever since he'd made the decision to come home. His family wasn't the main reason he'd come home, even though he was certainly happy to see them again.

The real reason was Susan.

Because until he saw her again, he would never be able to put the past behind him.

"You know, if I ever get out of this town, I'm never coming back!"

Susan Sheridan smiled at her neighbor, Amy Russell. "You always say that, but you love it here, you know you do."

Amy, a tall redhead, grinned. "I guess so."

The two women were sitting over iced tea and pretzels while their children played together in Susan's backyard pool. "What brought that on, anyway?" Susan said.

"Oh, I don't know." Amy thought a minute. "Actually, yes, I do. You know my sister Cathy is dating Glenn Callahan."

"Yes." At the mention of the Callahan name, Susan winced mentally, which irritated her. Her continued sensitivity where Keith's family was concerned was frustrating. After all, it had been more than ten years since she and Keith had had their one-night stand. You'd think she'd be immune to reminders of him by now.

"Well," Amy continued, "she happened to mention that Glenn's brother was coming back to Rainbow's End, and I guess that just made me think—" She broke off, frowning at Susan. "What's wrong?"

Susan gripped the edge of the table. "I—I suddenly felt faint." Her heart was beating like a tom-

tom in her chest. *Get ahold of yourself! Amy will think you're crazy!* She took several deep breaths.

Amy was already halfway out of her chair. "You look white as a sheet! Put your head between your legs. Are you sick?"

"No, no, I'm not sick. It—it's the heat."

"Well, then we'd better get you out of the sun."

"No, really, I'm okay." Susan took a drink of her tea, fanned herself with her hand, and gave Amy a weak smile.

"Are you sure?" Amy said.

Susan nodded. "Yes, I really am okay. I'm sorry. I didn't mean to scare you."

"Well, if you're sure…" Amy sat back down.

Susan forced herself to talk in a casual tone. "So you were saying Glenn Callahan's brother is coming back. Do you mean Keith?" Saying his name aloud made her heart pound again.

"Uh-huh. Do you know him?"

"Yes, I do. He was a good friend of Paul's. They went to school together."

"Oh. I didn't know that. Yeah, Keith's the one. Actually, I think he's the only Callahan who's left Rainbow's End. I mean, they're like the mainstay of the town."

Susan nodded, her mind whirling. Keith. Keith was coming home. Dear God. After all these years. All these years when she'd thought she was safe.

Her eyes moved to Scott, who was in the middle of the game of Marco Polo with Amy's two. Just then he laughed, the sound clear and joyous. A fierce love swept through her as she watched his dear face.

It was so good to hear him laugh again. He was finally beginning to heal after the grief of losing his beloved father.

She swallowed.

And now Keith was coming back.

And he would see Scott.

Scott, the son he didn't know he had.

Chapter Four

Susan calmed down after Amy and her children went home. That first unreasoning terror gave way to a more coolheaded awareness that she had over-reacted to the news of Keith's homecoming.

Just because Keith Callahan was coming back to Rainbow's End didn't mean she would see him. And even if she did see Keith, he wouldn't necessarily see Scott, too. And even if that remotely possible event took place, Keith would have no reason to sus-pect that Scott was his child and not Paul's.

After all, Scott had her light brown hair and freck-les. So what if his eyes were the same intense blue as Keith's? Lots of people had blue eyes. Paul's mother, for one.

Susan stared out her kitchen window. She tried not

to think how much Scott looked like Keith. From the time he was a toddler, she had lived in fear that someday Paul would see what she saw each time she looked at her son. The similarities between Scott and Keith were so obvious to her. It wasn't just the color of his eyes. He had the same-shaped face. The same nose. And the same irresistible smile.

Paul had had dozens of pictures of Keith. They were in his photo albums, on the wall of his study, all over the place.

And yet, after that first time, Paul had never questioned Scott's parentage.

Even now, Susan remembered the events leading up to Scott's birth as clearly as if they had only happened weeks, instead of years, before. The day after her shocking lapse of sense and judgment, when she realized Keith was gone, that what had happened between them hadn't meant anything to him except sex, that she would have to face Paul alone, she knew she could no longer continue to see him. She'd gone to Paul's apartment and gently told him it wasn't going to work.

At first, he didn't believe her.

"But why?" he'd said. "I don't understand."

"I just...I don't love you the way I should. I've known this for a long time, even though I didn't want to admit it. The thing is, you're such a good person, and I—I admire you. But I don't love you. I'm sorry."

The hurt in his eyes was like a knife in her chest. After a long moment, he said, "Is there someone else?"

She could hardly look him in the eyes, but she knew she must. *I love your best friend, and he doesn't love me.* If only she could tell him the truth. "No," she said. "There's no one else."

In the end, Paul had to accept what she told him, although he called her dozens of times over the next weeks and tried to persuade her to see him. But she remained firm. Eventually, he quit calling.

She missed him, though. She hadn't made many friends at school because she worked so much, and when she wasn't working, she was going to class or studying. Just about her only friend was Callie, her roommate, and Callie was hardly ever there.

Keith she tried not to think about.

She also tried not to castigate herself too much. Yes, she'd made a mistake. But breaking up with Paul would have been inevitable, anyway. What she and Keith had done had just made her decision easier.

Still, in the weeks following Keith's departure and her breakup with Paul, thoughts of Keith and the lovemaking they'd shared refused to be banished. Ruthlessly, she would shove them away again, angry with herself for a weakness that embarrassed her.

He doesn't love you, she reminded herself over and over again. *Stop thinking about him.*

It was a difficult time, compounded by the fact that she didn't feel well. Her stomach always seemed to be upset, and the smell of food at the restaurant where she worked aggravated the problem. In the mornings, it was all she could do to get out of bed.

And then she missed her period.

She told herself not to panic. There could be any number of reasons she was late. But it was hard not to be frightened, because Susan had never been late, not from the first month.

Suddenly the sickness she'd been enduring—a sickness she'd told herself was due to the stress she'd been under—made sense.

She bought a pregnancy kit, which confirmed what she already knew in her heart. She was pregnant. She was pregnant with Keith's child, for there had been no one else.

For a week, she walked around in a daze. What was she going to do? How could she have a baby? She was living from hand to mouth as it was. How could she support herself and a child and stay in school? And yet, if she didn't stay in school, she would never make a decent living, because she had very few marketable skills. And then she *really* wouldn't be able to take care of a child.

But what were her alternatives? The only one she would even consider was giving her child up for adoption. Yet the thought of doing so hurt. This was *her* child. But not just her child...

She swallowed.

Maybe she should tell Keith.

Her heart beat harder. The thought took root. Keith. They would be married. She would be Keith's wife. She even went so far as to pick up the phone and call directory assistance. She knew he lived with his parents. He'd laughed about it, saying something like, how many twenty-two-year-olds do you know who still live at home?

But she never made the call. Her good sense overrode her emotions. Yes, Keith probably *would* marry her, but did she really want him that way? For now she freely admitted to herself that she loved him. She had fallen in love with him practically from the first night they'd met, but she hadn't wanted to acknowledge it because of Paul.

And, of course, there was Paul to consider. Did she want to be responsible for the destruction of his friendship with Keith? Wasn't it bad enough what they had done to him?

If she had thought Keith loved her, she guessed she might have damned the consequences and faced up to her actions, but she was sure he didn't. No, what had happened between them that night was simply the result of lust on his part and weakness on hers.

The semester ended, Callie left for home, and Susan still hadn't made any kind of final decision. She did, however, give up her job at the restaurant and was lucky enough to find a full-time job clerking in a resale shop. The owner, Magda, was a generous, understanding woman who made allowances for Susan's condition.

Even though she wasn't sure how she would manage afterward, by midsummer Susan knew she wanted to keep the baby. Magda made the decision easier by offering Susan a nicer place to live: an apartment on the second floor of her home, which was located in a pleasant neighborhood of middle-class families. Susan cried when Magda made the offer. She knew her problems were far from solved, but at least she wouldn't have to bring the baby back to that ratty apartment complex. By the first of August, Susan was settled in her new place and beginning to feel better physically. She was also showing quite a bit. Luckily, Magda found her some used maternity outfits.

In mid-September, while running some errands, Susan had just put a quarter in a parking meter and was about to dash into the dry cleaner's to pick up some items belonging to the shop, when someone called her name. She turned, feeling the blood drain out of her face as she saw Paul coming toward her.

"Susan!" His glad smile faded as his eyes dropped to her protruding stomach.

"H-hello, Paul." Forcing herself to meet his eyes levelly, she willed herself to be calm. His expression said he was shocked. Deeply embarrassed, she tried to think what to say. "It...it's good to see you."

He swallowed. Cleared his throat. "It's good to see you, too."

For a few moments, they simply continued to regard each other awkwardly. Finally, looking at her stomach again, he said, "You're having a baby."

"Yes."

She could see he was stunned and trying not to show it. "Who's the lucky guy?" he finally said.

Answering him was the hardest thing she'd had to do in a long time. She sighed. "Who he is isn't important. It—it was a one-night stand, something I'm terribly ashamed of." And so saying, her eyes filled with tears.

"Susan." He touched her upper arm.

Please, God, help me. I don't want to break down in front of Paul. Please. "I'm sorry, Paul. I..." She tried to smile. "Pregnant women are awfully weepy. Don't pay any attention to me."

Now he seemed to regain his composure. The shock that had filled his hazel eyes had been replaced by concern. "Do you have a few free minutes? There's a Starbucks down at the corner. Let's go have something to drink, okay?"

Susan knew she shouldn't. Spending any more time with Paul was stupid. Dangerous, even. She was too vulnerable right now. What if she *did* break down? Oh, God. She couldn't. He could never, never know about Keith. Never. He thought the world of Keith. The knowledge of what she and Keith had done would destroy him.

Yet she was so glad to see him. She'd been so lonely since their breakup. She had so few friends, and the ones she did have weren't the kind of friends in whom you could confide. So she said yes.

They went to Starbucks. They sat for an hour, talking and catching up. Halfway through their conversation, Paul mentioned Keith. His expression was troubled. "He left Rainbow's End in April. It was a shock to everyone, including me. He never even said he was going, just up and left."

"Where'd he go?" She had the fleeting thought that what had happened between her and Keith was behind his abrupt departure, then immediately dismissed it. She was imagining herself a lot more important in his life than she actually was.

"Alaska."

''Have you talked to him?''

''Yeah. A couple of times.'' Paul frowned. ''I don't know. Something's wrong, but I don't know what. He just didn't act like the old Keith.'' And then his expression cleared. ''But listen, I don't want to talk about me. I want to talk about you.''

He asked her what she was going to do. She admitted she had no idea how she was going to manage when the baby was born. Her job at the resale shop certainly wouldn't support them both, especially when day care was so expensive. The minute the words were out of her mouth, she wished she hadn't said them. This wasn't Paul's problem, and she didn't want him worrying about her. But Paul had other ideas. He reached across the table and laid his hand over hers.

''Let me help you,'' he said softly.

The gentleness in his voice caused tears to threaten once more. She fought them, hating the way her emotions seemed to be so close to the surface. ''Paul, I—''

''Don't say anything. Just listen, okay? I love you. I've always loved you. Please let me help you. Marry me and let *me* be your baby's father.''

The unbelievably generous offer was her undoing. She started to cry. It was so tempting to say yes. To have someone with whom to share the responsibilities ahead. To have someone to lean on. But could she allow him to do this for her? He would be giving her so much, and she would be giving him nothing. She said as much.

And then he said something that stunned her. Because of the mumps he'd contracted his first year of college, he was now sterile. So she *would* be giving him something. She'd be giving him the son or daughter he'd always wanted. He said he'd intended to tell her long ago, but she'd broken up with him before he could.

"But what about your mother?"

"What *about* my mother?"

"Won't she despise me, knowing I'm pregnant with someone else's child?"

"She won't know. I'll tell her I'm the one who got you pregnant."

"But you said you were sterile."

Paul looked sheepish. "I never told my mother. I don't know why. I think I was ashamed."

His disclosure freed Susan and allowed her to accept his offer. They talked it over. Paul told her he hated law school. He'd never wanted to be a lawyer. He'd only done that to please his father. "And then," he added, "after I met you, I thought I could give you a better life if I was a lawyer. So I stuck with it."

"Oh, Paul."

He went on to say he wanted to move back to Rainbow's End. "The sheriff was a good friend of my father's. I know I can get a job with the department. And you'd love it there, Susan. It's a great town. Friendly. Pretty. Safe. A good place to raise kids." His eyes had implored her. "Say yes. I'll make you happy. I promise."

How could she refuse?

So Paul dropped out of school. Susan said goodbye to Magda. They packed up their belongings and moved. Three months later, on a cold, crisp December morning, their son Scott was born.

And he *was* Paul's son, Susan thought now. In every way that counted. And no matter what she had to do to keep the truth from surfacing, she would. Because no one could ever know Paul had not fathered Scott. After everything Paul had done for her and Scott, she owed Paul her silence and her loyalty.

But even if Paul's memory had not been a consideration, there was Laverne. From the very beginning, Paul's mother had been wonderful to Susan. Kind, accepting, and loving. In every way, she had taken the place of Susan's mother, and Susan loved her. And Laverne adored Scott. She would be devastated if she were to learn than Scott wasn't really her grandson. Laverne had already lost her only child. To lose her grandchild, too, would destroy her.

She would hate me, Susan thought. No. She couldn't bear it. The love and respect between Laverne and Susan meant too much to her. She would never do anything to jeopardize it.

And then there was the most important reason of all: Scott. Scott had had such a special, close relationship with Paul. The truth would turn Scott's world upside down. If he were to find out about Keith, he wouldn't understand. He might never forgive Susan for her deceit.

No.

Her secret must remain her secret.

Forever.

* * *

Keith slept late Monday morning and awakened to the smells of fresh coffee and cinnamon rolls. A quick shower and shave later, he sat at the worn kitchen table and wolfed down his mother's rolls along with a generous helping of scrambled eggs.

"If I keep eating like this I'll get fat," he complained, even as he accepted another buttery roll.

"Never," his mother said. "You're built just like your father, and he hasn't gained an ounce since the day we married." She grimaced, looking down at her rounded middle. "Not like me."

"You look great."

"I do not." But she was smiling.

After breakfast, Keith decided to visit some of his old haunts. Afterwards, he drove over to the construction site of a new elementary school on the south side of town. All of his brothers worked in the business and, except for Glenn, who was on vacation this week, were there. Keith felt a pang as he watched them working and laughing together. He enjoyed his job in Ketchikan, but he missed the closeness of working with family. His boss at the air-cargo company was an older, taciturn man who didn't offer much in the way of camaraderie.

After trading a few lighthearted remarks with his brothers, Keith headed for the office where he knew he would find his father and Sheila, who had recently begun working for him as his bookkeeper and office manager.

The outer office was empty, but Keith could see his father sitting at his desk in the inner office.

"Hey, Pop!"

His father looked up, a smile spreading across his face at the sight of Keith. "What are you doing here? C'mon in."

Keith shoved a pile of blueprints off the lone chair in the room and sat down. "Where's the squirt?" He inclined his head toward the outer office.

"She's gone to the dentist. What are you doing?"

"Just visiting."

"You planning to stay awhile?"

"Not really. Just thought I'd check things out."

They talked for a while, then Keith stood up.

"You on your way back to the house?" his dad asked.

Keith shrugged. "I don't know. Probably."

"Well, your mother just called and wanted me to stop at the store on the way home and get a few things for her. You want to do it instead?"

"Sure."

His father tore the top sheet off a small notepad and handed it to him. "This is the list."

Keith looked at it. Everything seemed clear.

"Here." His father had a wad of bills in his hand.

Keith refused to take the money, saying he could certainly pay for a few groceries. They talked a few more minutes, then Keith left.

It was a short, five-minute drive to the Kroger nearest the family home. Keith got a cart and slowly walked up and down the aisles as he tried to locate the items his mother wanted. When all that was left on the list were a few fruits and vegetables, he headed for the produce section. He had just tossed a bunch of bananas into his cart and was pushing it in the direction of the nectarine display when he saw her.

He sucked in a breath.

Susan.

She stood in front of a bin of fresh broccoli. She was in profile to him, so she didn't see him, and Keith was able to study her undetected. He was also able to regroup from his first shock at this unexpected encounter.

She looked beautiful to him. Her hair was the same shade of light brown, but now it had golden highlights, as if she spent a lot of time in the sun. It was shorter, too, brushed back and held up with some kind of big clip. Her dark green shorts and green-and-white-striped tank top showed off tanned arms and legs.

"Mom, look. Cherries. Can we get some?" From behind her a young, sandy-haired boy gestured.

Keith swallowed. Paul's son.

"Those are way too expensive, Scott," she said. And then she turned around.

Keith knew the exact moment when she recognized him, because she froze, and for just a moment something flickered in the depths of her eyes. He felt an overwhelming sense of regret as he walked toward her. What was she thinking? he wondered. Did she hate him? Or was what happened between them of so little importance to her now that she had all but forgotten it?

"Hello, Susan."

"Hello, Keith," she said pleasantly. Her smile was the reserved but friendly kind a woman would be expected to give an old friend of her husband's. "I heard you were back. When did you get in?"

"Yesterday." Tenderness welled in him. He hoped she *had* forgotten, because she was too good a person to have carried around a load of guilt for something that wasn't her fault.

"It's good to see you."

"It's good to see you, too. I...Susan, I'm so sorry about Paul."

She nodded, sorrow momentarily clouding her eyes. "Thank you."

Keith's gaze moved to her son, who had walked over to her side. Her arm went around him protectively. Now that he was closer, Keith could see the similarities between him and Susan. Same hair. Same freckles. He searched for signs of Paul, but the boy didn't resemble the Sheridans much. Obviously, he'd inherited his mother's genes. His bright blue eyes were studying Keith curiously.

"Keith, this is my son, Scott. Scott, this is Mr. Callahan. You know, your father's old friend."

Scott's eyes lit up. "Keith! My dad talked about you all the time!"

"Scott," Susan remonstrated, "we don't call adults by their first names."

Scott looked crestfallen, but only for a moment—his obviously natural exuberance preempting his embarrassment over being corrected by his mother. "Sorry, I—"

"No, it's okay. I want you to call me Keith." Keith looked at Susan. "As long as you don't mind."

She gave Scott an indulgent smile. "Well, if Keith says it's okay, I guess it's okay."

It was clear to Keith that Susan adored her son and that he, in turn, adored her. Something inside him ached for all that he had missed. Although Paul had died young, he'd been a lucky man while alive. These two were living proof of that.

"So how long are you planning to stay?" Susan asked, turning back to Keith.

"I don't know. A couple of weeks, at least."

"That's nice. I'll bet your mother's happy."

He smiled. "Yeah. If she has her way, I'll weigh three hundred pounds before I leave."

Susan laughed. "Paul told me about her cooking."

"And what about you? How are you doing?"

The smile faded. "I'm doing okay. It..." She glanced down at Scott. "It's been difficult, but we're better now."

"Listen, if there's anything, anything at all, that you need or I can do to help, all you have to do is call. I'm staying at my parents' house."

"That's nice of you, but we're fine. Really."

"Mom," Scott said, "what about that basketball hoop? Maybe Keith could put it up for me." His eyes were hopeful as they met Keith's.

"Scott..." she admonished.

"It's okay, Susan, I'd be glad to put up the hoop for you," Keith said.

"I hate—"

"No, don't worry about it." Keith smiled down at Scott. "Do you like basketball?"

"Yeah! I wanna be just like John Stockton when I grow up."

Susan made a face. "That's today. Tomorrow his hero will be Troy Aikman." She ruffled Scott's hair affectionately. Her eyes met Keith's again. "Are you sure you don't mind doing this?"

"I don't mind at all. It'll be fun. Who knows? Maybe Scott and I can shoot a few baskets afterward."

"That'd be cool!" Scott said. "Wouldn't it, Mom?"

There was an odd expression on Susan's face. But it disappeared quickly and her answer, when it came, was filled with amusement. "Yes, that would be cool."

"Good," Keith said, grinning. "How does tomorrow afternoon suit you?"

"If you can wait until after three, tomorrow afternoon is fine."

They agreed on four o'clock, and a few moments later parted company. As Susan and her son walked away, Keith resolved that during his time in Rainbow's End he would do everything in his power to help them. Maybe then he would finally be able to forgive himself.

Chapter Five

After exchanging greetings with Keith, Susan knew she should have said a quick goodbye and gone on her way. But somehow, even knowing how foolhardy it was to stand there, she had been incapable of leaving.

The trouble was, it was so good to see him. And she realized, in that moment when her heart gave a glad leap at the sight of him, that she had never forgotten him.

How could she? she thought wryly.

How could she even have *thought* she'd forgotten him? Especially when Scott was a daily reminder of that one night of passion?

Driving home from the supermarket with Scott, she couldn't concentrate on his chatter. Her mind played and replayed every word Keith had said, every gesture he'd made, every nuance of expression on his face.

She would have known him anywhere, even though there were significant differences in the way he looked now from the way he'd looked ten years ago. He was more mature looking, for one thing. A man instead of a boy. His hair was shorter, too, but still thick and wavy, with that blue-black sheen that had so fascinated her the first time she'd seen him.

And those eyes. Oh, God. Those eyes. They were Scott's eyes, and yet they weren't, for Scott's eyes were clear, young, innocent. There was nothing young or innocent about Keith's eyes. When he looked at her she had the feeling he could see right through her, just the way he had from the very beginning.

Her emotions had been chaotic, although she'd done her best to pretend the encounter hadn't affected her. She hoped she'd pulled it off. She would die if she thought Keith suspected what she was really feeling. After the first shock, her overriding emotion had been fear, even as she realized the fear was irrational. There was no way Keith could suspect the truth about Scott. And yet, when he'd looked at her son, she'd wanted to grab Scott and flee, she'd been that afraid.

She shouldn't have accepted Keith's offer to put up that basketball hoop tomorrow. It was stupid to spend time with him. It was playing with fire, because he still had the power to affect her in ways that were dangerous to her well-being. Ten years might have passed, but nothing had changed for her. She still wanted him. And she could never have him.

But how could she have said no to Scott? He was so eager, so happy about meeting Keith. And it was so good to see her son enthusiastic and carefree again. For too long, he had been hurting, and if seeing Keith made him feel better, she didn't want to be the one to take that good feeling away.

It's only one afternoon. I'm making too big a deal out of this. I handled today's encounter. I can handle tomorrow.

But that would be it, she decided as she turned the corner of their street. After tomorrow, she would not see Keith again. If Scott asked, she would make some excuse. And in a few weeks, there would no longer be a reason to worry. Keith would go back to Alaska, and she would never see him again.

Keith, along with the rest of his family, had been invited to dinner at Patrick Jr.'s home that evening.

"Wow," he said upon arrival. "You've remodeled."

"We had to," Patrick said. "We only had three bedrooms, and Jana really wanted a room of her own."

Jana was now fourteen and a budding beauty. In fact, Keith was a little stunned at how grown-up she looked. Girls grew up too fast nowadays, he thought. But she seemed like a nice girl. She was cheerfully helping her mother in the kitchen when he and Patrick walked to the back of the house.

"Hi, Keith," Jan said. Her face was flushed. Obviously, she'd been working hard, because the kitchen smelled wonderful and there was food in every stage of preparation on the counters and table-top.

"Hi, Uncle Keith," chorused his nieces. They were all working at something.

Allene, the youngest at six, stood on a stool. The tip of her tongue stuck out in concentration as she carefully spread butter on slices of French bread. "I'm making garlic bread," she said proudly.

"Ummm," Keith said. "Can I have a piece?" He reached toward the cookie sheet where she'd been placing the finished slices.

"No!" she said in a horrified tone. "They're not ready yet. They have to go in the oven."

"Oh, I see." Keith smothered his grin.

She rolled her eyes. "Men don't know anything."

She sounded so much like her mother, Keith couldn't help it. He laughed, and so did Patrick. Jan had a sheepish look on her face. "I wonder where she heard that," Keith said.

His other nieces grinned.

Katie, who was eleven, said, "Girls are just smarter than guys, that's all."

"I'll give you smarter," her father said.

"Patrick," Jan said, "why don't you get Keith something to drink and go on into the den? The others will be here soon."

"In other words," Patrick said, "she wants us to get out of the way."

Within the next twenty minutes, the remainder of the family had arrived, and soon the normal division—men in the den watching ESPN, women in the kitchen bustling about—was firmly established. Keith wondered if his family would ever join the nineties, and said as much.

"I help Jan all the time when we're alone," Patrick said indignantly. "In fact, I cook at least twice a week."

Everyone looked at Patrick Sr. to see what his reaction would be to this piece of information. He smiled. "I like to cook, too," he confessed. "But your mother doesn't like giving up control of her kitchen."

Keith and his brothers got a big kick out of this admission and teased his father for a while. During the affectionate ribbing, Sheila poked her head into the den to tell everyone dinner was ready. They all trooped into the dining room and were soon happily eating Jan's excellent Italian feast.

"Man, this is good stuff," Keith said around a mouthful of lasagna.

Jan smiled. "You need a wife."

"Him!" Rose said. "They *all* need wives."

"Not me," Rory said. "I'm too young to get married."

"Too young!" Patrick Sr. said. "I was only twenty-five when I got married, and you're twenty-nine already."

"Things are different now," Rory said, looking at his brothers, who murmured agreement.

"Yeah," Sheila said dryly. "Men are totally selfish and self-involved now, that's what's different."

"Now, Sheila," her mother said. "That's not true."

"You're not out there dating, Ma," Sheila said. "Believe me, it's true."

"I don't think I'm selfish and self-involved," Kevin said in a mock-injured tone.

"No, you're not selfish," Sheila returned, "you think driving a BMW convertible and going to Aruba every six months is your just due."

"Hey, I work hard for my money. If I want to spend it that way, it's my business."

"Yeah," echoed Rory.

"Besides," Kevin said, "you can talk all you want about men, Sheila, but it's not easy to find the kind of woman I want."

"Which is?" Sheila said.

"Someone just like Ma." Kevin grinned triumphantly.

"Oh, spare me," Sheila said, rolling her eyes.

Keith chuckled. He realized he'd missed his family's spirited disagreements. "Hey, squirt," he said to Sheila, "you sound like you're jealous of us guys."

"Jealous! Why, I wouldn't be a man for all the tea in China. Everyone knows women are more intelligent. And don't call me 'squirt'!"

"Okay, squirt." He laughed when she wadded up her napkin and pretended she was going to throw it at him, and after a minute, she laughed, too.

"So *you're* the one who's corrupted my nieces."

Sheila frowned. "*What* are you talking about?"

Keith explained about the conversation in the

kitchen before dinner. Then the rest of his brothers got into the act, and before long insults were flying back and forth, with Katie and Jana joining in to help their Aunt Sheila.

"To bring this conversation back to an *intelligent* level," Sheila finally said, turning to her mother, "I saw Laverne Sheridan at the pharmacy this afternoon. I was shocked. She looks terrible."

"Poor thing," Rose said, her eyes turning soft with sympathy. "She's taking Paul's death hard. I can't imagine what it must be like to lose a child, let alone your only child."

Sheila nodded. "I know. I felt so sorry for her. I'll bet she's lost at least twenty pounds, and she couldn't afford to lose five."

"Yeah," Rory chimed in. "I saw her last week and hardly recognized her. She looks years older."

Rose shook her head sadly. "It's such a shame. But thank God for her grandson." She gave her granddaughters a loving look. "Because as long as she has him, she'll always have a part of Paul."

"I saw him today," Keith said. "He's a cute kid."

"Yes, he is," his mother said. She looked at Keith curiously. "Did you go over there? To Paul's house, I mean?"

"No, I ran into Susan at Kroger when I was picking up that stuff for you."

"Oh. I didn't realize you knew Susan."

"I met her before she and Paul got married. You know. That time I went to Austin and spent spring break with Paul."

"Oh, that's right. I'd forgotten about that. Well,

she's a lovely young woman. Laverne thinks the world of her.''

"Good-looking, too," Kevin said.

"That's what lovely means," Sheila said sweetly.

"Not necessarily," Kevin said. "It could mean she's nice. That's what you meant, Ma, isn't it?"

Rose sighed. "Not another argument, okay?"

"I didn't start it," Kevin said.

"Enough," Patrick Sr. said. "We all agree. Susan Sheridan is a very nice, very pretty woman, and it's sad that she's lost her husband at such a young age."

Kevin obediently turned his attention back to his food, but not before winking at Keith and saying, "See what you've been missing all these years?"

The talk turned to something else then, and Keith was grateful, because he'd felt uncomfortable throughout the exchange. Silly to feel that way, he knew, but he'd never liked concealing things from his family.

He kept thinking about what Sheila and Rory and his mother had said, though, especially about Paul's mother. He decided that, even though it would be difficult, he would go to see Laverne in a couple of days.

For the rest of the meal, the talk was general and pleasant. Then, while they were in the middle of dessert—a rich chocolate cake loaded with pecans—his father turned to Keith. "I know you said you weren't sure how long you're going to be here, Keith, but I wish you'd think about staying permanently. We could sure use you in the business. Things are booming around here, and you know how I don't like to hire outsiders. It's much better to keep the work in the family.''

"You hired Jack Kinsella," Sheila said.

"Jack is practically family," Kevin said. Jack Kinsella was his best friend.

"Well, I *am* family, and he wouldn't hire me!"

"Sheila, please," Patrick Sr. said, "we've gone over this at least a hundred times, and I'm not going to change my mind. A construction crew is no place for a woman."

"It's okay for me to be in the *office*, though," Sheila grumbled.

"That's different. Being in the office isn't dangerous. And the language is a lot cleaner."

"You know, Dad, I'm a grown woman. I can take care of myself."

Patrick Sr.'s face closed into stubborn lines. "I don't want to discuss this further, Sheila."

Keith looked at his sister. For a moment, he thought she was going to continue to press their father, but then her lips tightened into a stubborn scowl that matched her father's, and she slumped into silence. Keith bit back a smile. His fiery sister always amused him, but he felt sorry for the guy she eventually married. She sure would lead *him* a merry chase.

"Well, Keith?" His father turned to him again. "Will you think about what I said?"

"Yeah, Pop, I will." He looked around the table. All the adults were looking at him, and in every pair of eyes except Sheila's—she was still scowling—he saw hope. He threw up his hands. "Okay. Okay. I'll give it a *lot* of thought."

Scott had a doctor's appointment at two o'clock Tuesday, and it was three-thirty before they got back home. Susan was glad she'd told Keith to come at four. She would have hated for him to have to sit and wait on them.

"I'm gonna go change clothes," Scott said. "'Cause I want to help Keith put up that hoop."

"All right. While you do that, I'll make some lemonade for you guys to drink, because it's hot out there." She debated changing her own clothes, then decided not to.

Keith arrived a few minutes before four. Susan's pulse quickened at the sight of him, which first exasperated her, then made her feel guilty. What was wrong with her? Even if there weren't other complications, Paul had only been dead eight months, and here she was, acting like a giddy teenager.

But Keith *did* look so handsome! she thought as he walked toward the house. He was wearing khaki shorts with lots of pockets and a bright blue T-shirt that revealed his taut physique. Suddenly, she was very glad she hadn't changed clothes and was still wearing the short brown linen sheath she'd worn to the doctor's office, because she knew it showed off her legs to advantage.

As Keith neared the door, she quickly moved away from the window so he wouldn't know she'd been watching him. Taking a deep breath, she composed her face before answering the doorbell.

"Hi," he said, smiling.

Her traitorous heart refused to beat calmly, especially in the face of that killer smile. "Hi. Come on in. Scott's upstairs."

Keith started to say something, but Scott, obviously hearing his arrival, came flying down the stairs. "Keith! You're here!"

Keith grinned. "Ready to get started?"

"I sure am!"

Susan hadn't heard this kind of enthusiasm from Scott since before Paul's death, and once again, she knew she'd made the right decision yesterday. Hard as it was for her to be in Keith's company, this was the right thing for Scott. And Scott's well-being was a lot more important than her feelings.

"Well, come on, let's go get my tools out of the truck, okay? And then you can show me where the hoop is."

"Okay!"

They took off, and a few minutes later Susan carried the pitcher of lemonade outside and put it and a couple of glasses on the umbrella table by the pool. Then she walked out the gate to the garage.

"Susan. What do you think? Should I put the hoop here?" Keith pointed to the middle of the garage.

"I don't care. Whatever you think."

"Is that where you normally park your car?" He indicated the open garage, where her car was parked on the right side.

"Yes."

"Well, maybe you'd rather the hoop go over here on the left side, then."

"It really doesn't matter. Wherever it is, it isn't going to interfere with my parking."

"You sure?"

"Yes."

"In that case, I think it'll look better in the middle."

Once that was decided and Susan asked him if there was anything else he needed, she told them where the lemonade was, then went back into the house. She decided she would get started making a pot of chili for dinner, which meant she could unobtrusively watch Keith and Scott work from the kitchen window that overlooked the driveway.

Taking her Dutch oven out, she poured in a little olive oil, then got busy chopping onions. It took longer than usual, because she kept stopping and looking out the window. It was nice to watch Keith work. He obviously knew what he was doing. Paul hadn't been very handy around the house, even though he'd tried. She was glad to see that Keith really was allowing Scott to help him. She knew Scott must be thrilled. Several times, she heard his laughter ring out. The laughter was good to hear, and yet in some way she couldn't understand, it hurt her, too. The hurt was all tied up with Paul and how much he'd loved Scott and the guilt she'd never been able to banish.

When she finally finished chopping the onions, she heated the oil, then dumped in the onions, followed by ground turkey. Her mind still on the two males outdoors, she browned the meat and onions. Once that was done, she added the remaining ingredients and seasoned the mixture, then left it on low heat to simmer.

She knew it wasn't wise to go back outside, but she couldn't seem to help herself. Keith was like a magnet, drawing her to him when he was anywhere near. After smoothing back her hair, she opened the back door and walked out to the driveway. Keith was just coming down the ladder, and the hoop was up.

"Well, I think that's it." He smiled at Scott, who beamed back. "Want to try it out, shoot a few baskets?"

"Yeah!" Scott said.

The look on his face as he ran into the house to get his basketball was worth any amount of discomfort Susan was feeling.

After he'd gone, her eyes met Keith's. "Thank you," she said softly.

He shrugged. "No big deal."

"Yes, it was. You made a little boy awfully happy."

"I was glad to do it. He's really a nice kid."

She smiled. "Yes, I think so."

Glancing away from her, he said slowly, "You and Paul, you did a great job with him."

Without warning, Susan's eyes filled with tears.

"Well, if there's anything else you can think of—" Looking up, he broke off. "Susan, what... what's wrong?"

Embarrassed, she brushed the tears away. "Nothing. There's nothing wrong."

"Are you sure?"

She nodded. "I just…it was just the reminder of Paul, I guess."

Just then Scott came through the gate. He held his basketball.

Grateful for the diversion, Susan said, "Looks like Scott's ready."

"Go ahead," Keith said. "Let's see you shoot one."

Scott missed on his first try but made the next one. Then Keith took a few shots. Soon he was showing Scott how to play one-on-one.

Susan went inside to check on her chili and make a salad. By the time she was finished, her emotions were back on an even keel. She wanted to go back outside, but she forced herself not to. Instead, she sat down at the kitchen table and leafed through the new edition of *Cooking Light* magazine, which was one of her favorites. But as much as she loved the magazine, she couldn't seem to concentrate on the articles, because she could hear the bounce and thwack of the ball as it hit the concrete and the laughter and good-natured shouts accompanying the game of one-on-one.

It was only when the game was over and she heard them come into the backyard that she went out to join them. Keith had downed one glass of lemonade and was pouring another. Sweat had soaked his T-shirt, and his face was red. Scott looked just as hot and wet.

"I'll go get some towels so you guys can dry off," she said. When she returned with the towels, the two of them had gone back out to the driveway. She walked out and saw Keith standing inside the garage. She handed him a towel and gave Scott the other one.

"What're these?" he said, drying his face. He pointed to some boxes stacked against the inner wall.

"Oh, just some mini-blinds that I have to get installed." Susan had been meaning to call the man who did that kind of thing for her but hadn't gotten around to it.

"Where are they going to go?"

"In the front bedroom."

"I can put them in for you."

"Oh, no. You've done enough."

"Susan, it won't take me thirty minutes to install these." Without waiting for her to answer, he picked up the boxes. "Scott, bring my toolbox, okay?" He looked at Susan again. "Show me where."

Later she would wonder what possessed her to say what she said next. But at the moment, the words just seemed to come out of her mouth with no direction from her. "The only way I'm going to let you do this is if you let me pay you back by feeding you. I made a big pot of chili. Will you stay and have dinner with us?"

"Yeah, Keith!" Scott said. "Stay and have dinner with us."

Keith's eyes met hers. "I'm all sweaty."

"We don't care!" Scott said.

"No big deal," she said, echoing his earlier words.

"Well, in that case..." He grinned. "You don't have to ask me twice. Chili is one of my favorite meals."

While he was upstairs installing the blinds, Susan got the table ready downstairs. She told herself there was no harm in him staying for dinner. Her paranoia of the day before had been ridiculous. After all, he didn't suspect anything.

And as long as she didn't give him any reason to, he never *would* suspect anything.

Chapter Six

Keith drilled the last of the holes needed to install the final blind, and five minutes later he was finished. He tested the blind, making sure it opened and closed easily. When it checked out, he turned to Scott, who had been helping him by handing him things.

"Well, that's it. Let's get these tools put away, then I guess we'd better wash up."

Scott's eager agreement gave Keith a warm feeling. He really was a nice kid. Paul must have been proud of him. What a dirty shame it was that Paul had died so young, leaving Scott without a father to look up to and do things with. At least if the kid had grandfathers or uncles—some male figure in his life—it wouldn't be so bad. But there was no one. Now if Keith was going to *stay* in Rainbow's End...

The moment the thought reared its head, Keith dismissed it as being presumptuous, not to mention egotistical. He was probably the *last* person Susan would want hanging around as a constant reminder of their youthful folly.

"I'll show you where the bathroom is," Scott said as they finished packing up Keith's tools.

Once they were cleaned up, they headed down to the kitchen, where Susan was putting the finishing touches to the table. Up till now, Keith had been too interested in the home's occupants to pay much attention to his surroundings, but now he looked around admiringly.

Funny, he thought, how you could always tell a woman's kitchen versus a man's. This kitchen definitely had a woman's touch. It looked cheerful and homey with yellow print wallpaper, white cupboards and countertops, and several healthy-looking plants dotting the windowsills. In the center of the room was a round, light-oak table, festively set with dark turquoise dishes.

Susan looked up as they walked in. Her face was becomingly flushed, her eyes bright. He realized she was even more attractive now than she'd been ten years ago. And he also realized he wanted her every bit as much now as he had then. He knew the thought was inappropriate and tried to push it away.

"Everything's just about ready," she said.

"Table looks nice."

She smiled. "Thanks." She pointed to one of the chairs. "Have a seat."

"Do you mind if I use the phone first?" Keith had

belatedly remembered his mother would be expecting him for dinner.

"No, of course not. Um, if you'd like some privacy, there's a phone in the study. Scott, show him where it is."

Keith followed Scott down the hall and into a small room at the side of the house that was furnished with a walnut desk, leather chairs, and bookcases. Paul's room, he thought, looking at the pictures of hunting dogs that adorned the walls. Then he saw the picture of himself, Paul, and Paul's father. With a wrench of sadness, he remembered how much he and Paul used to enjoy going hunting with Paul's dad. Keith wondered if Paul had ever taken Scott hunting, and regret filled him once more for all the things Paul and Scott would never do together.

"There's the phone," Scott said.

Shaking off his melancholy thoughts, Keith smiled at the boy. "Thanks."

Scott politely left him alone then, and Keith called home. Once that was taken care of, he rejoined Scott and Susan in the kitchen. Scott was already seated, and Susan was spooning chili into a bowl for him.

"Hand me your bowl, Keith." She filled his bowl, then hers. Keith waited until she was ready to sit down before taking his place.

"We always say grace," Susan said, reaching for Scott's hand.

"So does my family," Keith said. A little self-consciously, he reached for Scott's other hand, then offered his right hand to her. Her eyes met his briefly as she slipped her hand into his.

She said a short prayer, and even though Keith tried to concentrate on the words, he was too conscious of the feel of hers and Scott's hands, too aware of how good it was to be here with them, and too mindful of how much he'd missed all these years and how much Paul would miss in all the years to come.

But whatever sadness he felt was quickly banished once they began to eat, because Scott eagerly asked Keith to tell him about his years in Alaska.

Keith described the state—the forests and mountains—and what it was like to fly through the fjords. He told them how a person could travel hundreds of miles without seeing another human being.

"It sounds so cool," Scott said.

"It *does* sound lovely," Susan said.

"It's an unbelievably beautiful place," Keith said. "But it can be lonely."

"Did you ever see any bears?" Scott said. A typical kid, he wasn't interested in discussions of loneliness.

Keith smiled. "Yes. A couple of times. But I stayed away from them. Bears are dangerous."

"I know. We read about them in school. Man, they're *huge!*"

"Yes, they are."

"And my teacher said they can run really fast."

"That's true," Keith said. "Some people have made the mistake of thinking they could outrun a bear. Believe me, you can't."

"What kind of a place do you live in?" Susan asked.

"I rent an apartment. Three rooms over a store."

"Really?"

"Yep. There's a souvenir shop on the first floor and my apartment upstairs. The guy who owns the store used to live in it, but then he got married and they had a baby, so they built a little house and moved. I like it. It's right on the main street."

"Souvenirs?" Susan said. "I thought you lived in a remote area."

"Ketchikan's a port, and most of the big cruise ships dock there for a few hours on their way up the inside passage, so we get lots of tourists during the summer. In fact, the tourist trade is a large part of the town's income. So in that sense, we're not remote."

She nodded and for the first time since they'd started eating, silence fell between them. Scott broke it by saying, "What's for dessert, Mom?"

"There are some chocolate-chip cookies left."

"Oh, good. Where are they?"

"In the pantry. You'll see. I put them in a plastic container." Susan turned to Keith. "How about you? Can I interest you in some cookies? They're homemade."

Keith patted his stomach. "Thanks, but I've been eating too much since I got here. I think I'll pass." He smiled. "Thanks for the dinner, Susan. It was great."

"You're welcome. I appreciate your coming over and putting up the hoop and..." She broke off, glancing toward the window that faced the driveway. "Someone's here."

Keith heard the clunk of a car door, then the creak

of the side gate opening and closing. A few seconds later, there was a knock at the kitchen door.

"It's Gran!" shouted Scott, jumping up.

Susan pushed her chair back and stood.

Scott ran to the door and opened it. "Gran! Hi!"

Keith slowly got to his feet and watched as Laverne Sheridan bent to hug Scott. Keith could see that his sister and brother had been right. Even making allowances for the more than ten years that had passed since he'd seen Paul's mother, the changes in her were glaring. Why, she looks like an old woman, he thought, and she was actually a few years younger than his own mother, who looked great for sixty-one. As Laverne straightened, her gaze landed on Keith. Shock, followed by a glimmer of something else, flared in her eyes. For a moment, Keith had the crazy thought the emotion he'd seen was fear, but it was gone so fast he told himself he'd imagined it.

"Mom," Susan said, "you remember Keith Callahan, don't you?"

"Yes, of course. I heard you were home, Keith. How are you?"

She smiled, but Keith sensed a lack of warmth in the smile, even though her voice and expression were completely pleasant. He guessed if she wasn't overjoyed to see him, he could understand the reason. In her eyes, he hadn't been much of a friend to Paul the past ten years.

"I'm fine, Mrs. Sheridan. How are you?"

The smile faded, and she shrugged. "As well as can be expected, I suppose."

"I was sorry to hear about Paul," Keith said awkwardly.

She nodded, biting her lower lip. The bleakness in her eyes was painful to see.

Susan had moved to Laverne's side. She put her arm around her mother-in-law and kissed her cheek. "Have you eaten? There's lots of chili left."

"Thank you, dear, but I'm not hungry."

"Now, Mom, you have to eat."

Laverne started to say something, then sighed. "Oh, all right. I'll have a small bowl. *Small*," she emphasized.

Susan smiled. "Good. Sit down." She indicated the extra chair.

Laverne put her purse down and walked over to the table, but she didn't sit. She looked at Keith again. "How long are you going to be in Rainbow's End, Keith?"

"I'm not sure. A couple of weeks, probably."

Susan placed a steaming bowl on the table in front of Laverne. "Here's your chili."

While his mother had been fixing his grandmother's food, Scott had gone to the pantry. Now he came back to the table with the plastic container of cookies. He sat down and Paul's mother followed suit. Keith decided it might be a good idea for him to leave. It was obvious to him that Laverne Sheridan was not overjoyed to see him, and he'd just had the unpleasant realization that part of the reason for her lack of enthusiasm might be because she thought he was trying to make a move on Susan. But no sooner had the thought formed than he dismissed it. It was probably just his own guilty conscience that had planted *that* idea. Even so, it was time to go.

"Susan, I'm going to be on my way. Thanks again for dinner."

"Oh, do you *hafta* go?" Scott said, disappointment written all over his face.

Keith smiled down at him. "Yeah, I'm afraid I do."

"But you're gonna come back, aren't you? 'Cause we gotta play one-on-one again."

Keith hesitated. He wanted to say yes. He liked Scott a lot, yet he wasn't sure how Susan would feel about him spending more time with the boy. "We'll see," he hedged. He turned to Susan. "Remember, if you need anything else done around here in the next couple of weeks, just give me a call."

"Thanks, Keith. I appreciate that."

Finally, he addressed Paul's mother. "Goodbye, Mrs. Sheridan. It was good to see you again."

"Goodbye, Keith." She didn't smile.

As he walked out the door, he knew one thing for certain. If Paul's mother had anything to do with it, this was the last time Keith would ever set foot in Susan's house.

Susan was mystified by her mother-in-law's behavior. Normally a warm, friendly woman, she'd obviously been less than thrilled to see Keith. Was something wrong?

"How did Keith happen to be here for dinner?" Laverne said as soon as the door closed behind him.

"We ran into him at Kroger yesterday and he offered to put up the basketball hoop for Scott. You know, the one I ordered from the Sears catalog.'' Susan tried not to sound defensive, but her mother-in-law's tone and the almost accusatory look in her eyes made it difficult not to.

"Yeah," said Scott around a mouthful of cookie. "And I helped him! It was cool. And then we played one-on-one. And then Keith and me installed the blinds Mom bought. He let me hold the drill and showed me how to put the screws in and everything! You should see his toolbox, Gran. He's got *everything*. He told me before he went to Alaska he used to work for his father and build houses and schools and everything. He worked on *my* school, he said." All of this information was delivered so fast that half his words ran together.

It was clear to Susan that Scott had a bad case of hero-worship. She only wished he hadn't shown it so plainly to his grandmother, because she was afraid Laverne would view his enthusiasm as some sort of disloyalty to Paul. Although why she should, Susan didn't know.

Laverne nodded. "I see." But when her eyes met Susan's a moment later, it wasn't sadness or hurt that Susan saw in their blue depths. Instead, there was a cool, speculative gleam.

Susan knew she had done nothing wrong, but she couldn't stop the creeping feelings of guilt or the sudden awareness that Laverne might actually be thinking that it wasn't only Scott who was enamored of Keith, but that Susan, too, might be thinking of him as a replacement for Paul. "It was very nice of

Keith to offer to put up the hoop and install the mini-blinds for us." This time the words *did* sound defensive, but Susan couldn't help it.

"Yes," Laverne said, "very nice." But the words didn't carry the ring of sincerity and the speculative gleam remained, even as she picked up her spoon and took a bite of her chili.

"Mom," Scott said, totally oblivious to the undertones between his mother and his grandmother. He shoved his chair back. "I'm done. Can I go play my new PlayStation?"

"Sure," Susan said, relieved that he was going. The last thing she wanted was for him to sense any discord between her and Laverne.

The moment they heard his footsteps on the stairs, Laverne said, "You know, Susan, if you need anything else done around here that you can't do yourself, just let me know. I'll send John over." She was referring to the handyman/gardener who worked for her a couple of days each week.

Susan nodded, even though she had no intention of letting Laverne take care of things that she herself needed to take care of. But it was easier to pretend to agree than to get into a debate over the subject.

"I'd much rather John do things for you than have you obligated to anyone else," Laverne added.

Although she had obviously tried to make her comment sound casual, Susan detected a certain edge to the words. After a few seconds' debate on how to answer, Susan said, "I don't feel *obligated* to Keith. I think, because of Paul, it made Keith feel good to do something for Scott."

Laverne shrugged. "Yes, well…"

There was definitely something else going on here, something other than what her mother-in-law had said. You didn't have to be a brain surgeon to see that Laverne didn't approve of Keith and didn't want Susan and Scott to have anything to do with him.

"…that's enough of that," Laverne continued. "Let's talk about something much more pleasant. Have you given any more thought to the California trip?"

Laverne wanted to take Susan and Scott with her to California in October. She was planning to visit her oldest friend and thought it would be good for all of them to get away. Susan hadn't agreed yet, because it bothered her to take Scott out of school for an entire week, even though he was an excellent student and could probably make up the work without any difficulty. But now, Susan had another reason for declining the offer, and she'd been putting off telling her mother-in-law about it, because she knew her news would upset Laverne.

"Yes," she said, "I've thought about it, but… well, I'm afraid we won't be able to go with you."

"Susan, why not? You're not still worried about Scott, are you? It won't hurt him to miss a week of school. We'll have such a great time. Frances has all kinds of things planned for us. Things he'll adore. A day at Disneyland. A day at Universal Studios. He'll have a wonderful time and he'll learn a lot."

Susan sighed. Laverne was right. It *wouldn't* hurt Scott to miss a week of school. "Okay, Mom, you're right. Scott can go. But I can't.'' Before her mother-in-law could protest, Susan rushed on. ''You see, I...last week I interviewed for a job and...and yesterday morning I found out I got it.''

''A job!'' Laverne was clearly flabbergasted. ''You're not serious. What kind of a job?''

Susan smiled. She felt a tremendous relief now that she'd finally told Laverne. ''I'm going to be Tom Shaver's assistant.'' Tom was the dean of the local community college and an old friend of Paul's late father's. ''I'm starting next week.''

Laverne shook her head. ''Susan, this is crazy. You don't need to work. There's plenty of money. You know that.''

''It's not entirely about money,'' Susan said gently. ''Please try to understand, Mom. I need to do something. I need to feel productive. But even if I didn't, I couldn't take your money.''

''But Susan, whatever I have, it would have been Paul's someday, anyway. And now it's going to be yours and Scott's.''

Susan sighed. She reached for Laverne's hand and stroked it softly. ''I love you for offering to help me. But I have to make my own way.''

''But...but what about Scott?''

''I've enrolled him in Molly Callahan's program.'' Molly was married to Jim Callahan, a cousin of Keith's, and ran an after-school and summer program for children ages six through twelve whose mothers worked. Everyone Susan had talked to had nothing but glowing things to say about both Molly and her program.

"Oh, Susan, no!" Laverne said. "Not day care. If you really *must* go to work, I'll watch Scott."

Before answering, Susan steeled herself. She had known this was what Laverne would say. Again she spoke very gently. "We both know that wouldn't work. Scott needs to be around other children. But more than that, he'd wear you out."

For a long moment, Laverne stared at her. Then, like a balloon whose air has been let out, she seemed to shrink. She put down her spoon and sank back in her chair. Her lower lip trembled. "I hate this," she whispered with stricken eyes. "I hate this. Paul should be here. Then none of this would be happening."

Susan's own eyes filled with tears. She got up and knelt by Laverne's chair. Putting her arms around her mother-in-law, she said, "I know."

"It's so unfair," Laverne cried in a muffled voice. "No mother should ever outlive her child."

"I know," Susan repeated. Laverne was right. Outliving a child was against the laws of nature. She wished she could think of something comforting to say to her mother-in-law, but everything had been said dozens of times. Besides, what good were platitudes? Paul was gone, and nothing would change that fact. And yet, Susan had to try, because she loved Laverne and couldn't stand seeing her so unhappy. "It *is* unfair, but Paul wouldn't want you to grieve like this. You know he wouldn't."

For a long moment, Laverne didn't answer. Finally she gave a long, shuddering sigh, sniffed and moved away from Susan's embrace. "I know. I'm sorry."

Her eyes met Susan's and she made a brave attempt to smile. "I love you, Susan. You were a wonderful wife to Paul and you're a wonderful mother to Scott. And you've been a wonderful daughter to me."

Susan's throat was almost too full to speak. Still she managed to say, "I love you, too."

As the two women hugged, Susan felt the weight of her responsibility to this woman who had been so good to her and had taken her into her heart so completely.

In that moment, she vowed she would never, ever do anything to hurt Laverne. And if keeping that vow meant not seeing Keith again, then somehow Susan would have to find a way to explain the situation to Scott.

Keith thought about Susan and Scott all the way home. He wished...hell, he didn't know *what* he wished. He guessed he wished things could be different. That Susan was free and he was free and he could see her without feeling guilty about it. Trouble was, they would never be free of the past. The past existed, and now Paul's shadow would always be between them.

So forget about her. You saw her. You saw that she's okay, that she doesn't hold any kind of grudge against you, and you did what you could to show her you're sorry about everything. Now it's time to move on.

But no matter what he told himself, he couldn't seem to put Susan *or* Scott out of his mind. He was still thinking about them when he pulled up in front of his parents' home.

Walking inside, he found Rory there.

"'Bout time you got home," Rory said. "I've been waiting over an hour."

"What're you doing here? Don't you have a home of your own?" Keith countered.

"I thought maybe we could go lift a few at Pot O' Gold." Pot O' Gold was the local hangout for their old gang.

That was a good idea. Maybe then he'd be able to forget about Susan. "Sure. Sounds good. Just let me get cleaned up and change my clothes. Shouldn't take more than thirty minutes."

"We'll walk," Rory said. "That way, if we have a few too many, we won't have to worry about driving. I can always crash here tonight, can't I, Ma?"

True to his word, Keith was ready to go a half hour later. Keith's parents lived a short six-block walk to the downtown area of Rainbow's End, which was where Pot O' Gold was located. It was a pleasant stroll now that the sun had gone down, so the brothers didn't hurry.

"Guess who's working at Pot O' Gold now," Rory said.

"Who?"

"Kitty O'Brien."

"Really?" Kitty O'Brien had been in the same high school graduating class as Keith, and he'd dated her for a short period of time just before his twentieth birthday. "I haven't thought about Kitty in years. How's she doing?"

"She's had some ups and downs. You know she married Doug Paglia."

"No, I didn't know that." Doug was another ex-classmate of Keith's, but he'd run around with a faster crowd than Keith had ever cared to be associated with.

"Yeah. I guess he knocked her around some before she finally threw him out. Then a year later he got busted for dealing cocaine."

"No kidding? That's too bad."

"Anyway, Kitty's been at Pot O' Gold for a couple of years now. Big Jim really thinks a lot of her." Big Jim Sullivan was the owner of the pub and a friend of Patrick Sr. "She's still a looker, too." He grinned. "I told her you were coming home, and she was *real* interested."

"Oh, yeah?" Maybe that's what Keith needed. A good-looking woman to take his mind off another good-looking woman who was off-limits.

By now they'd reached the pub. When Keith and Rory walked in, they were greeted enthusiastically by a rowdy crowd. There was a lot of backslapping and good-to-see-you-agains for Keith.

"Hey, Rory, Keith, over here!" someone yelled.

Rory grinned. "Kevin and Sean are here."

Keith craned his neck to see, and sure enough, there were their two brothers in the back of the room. It took Keith a while to get there, though, because along the way he kept seeing people he knew and had to stop and talk. Finally he made it to the table, where Rory was already seated.

"So you guys still hang out here, huh?" Keith said.

Sean shrugged. "There's not exactly a lot to do in this town at night."

"On weekends, we go into Austin a lot," Kevin said, "but during the week, this is the place to be."

Keith looked around. Not much had changed over the years. There were still three dartboards mounted, with people playing games at each one. And there was still a piano player and a bunch of people gathered around him, singing old songs. The only difference was the addition of a big-screen TV near the bar, but how anyone could hear it over the din was a mystery to Keith.

While he was still looking around, he saw a waitress weaving her way through the tables. He smiled as he recognized Kitty O'Brien. When she got closer, he stood.

"Keith! Hi!"

She reached up to hug him. Rory had been right, he thought as they drew apart. She was still a looker, with shoulder-length red-gold hair and a great body.

"Rory told me you were coming home." Her smile said she was very glad to see him.

"Hello, Kitty. You're looking good."

"So are you. You're looking *very* good." She gave him a slow, provocative once-over. Behind him, his brothers chuckled.

The invitation in her eyes should have made Keith feel terrific. But all he felt was the normal pleasure of seeing an old friend.

Yes, she was a looker. And, yes, she was sexy.

And, yes, most men would be salivating over her and planning how they could get her into their bed.

But unfortunately for him, his head was filled with the image of a brown-eyed woman with a sweet smile and a husky voice.

A woman he didn't have a chance in hell of ever winning.

A woman who just might have forever spoiled him for anyone else.

Chapter Seven

On Monday, Susan took extra pains with her appearance. Giving herself one last check in the mirror, she decided she looked competent and professional. Yes, the dark jade linen suit paired with the pale aqua shell was perfect, as were her bone heels and off-white hose. She gave one last pat to her hair, then picked up her purse and headed for Scott's bedroom.

"You ready, honey?" she said, poking her head in.

Scott was sitting on the end of his bed lacing up a sneaker. "Uh-huh." He finished with the shoe and reached for his backpack, which contained his swimsuit and assorted belongings.

"Let's go, then."

The drive to Molly's Before & After didn't take

long. Although in the future Susan would drop Scott under the porte-cochere, since this was his first day, she walked inside with him.

Molly Callahan, a tall blonde with kind eyes, smiled as they entered the big, open classroom. "Hi, Scott. Welcome."

"Hi," Scott said, although his eyes lit up when he spied a friend of his who was already there. The boy, whom Susan recognized as Travis Webber, a classmate of Scott's, waved.

"You can put your things in your locker," Molly said, indicating the row of lockers at the far end of the room. "I marked your name on it."

Susan knew Scott would be embarrassed if she hugged him, so she just smiled and said, "'Bye, honey. See you this afternoon."

"'Bye, Mom."

It surprised Susan that she felt such a wrench leaving him. He hadn't acted as if he minded going to the day-care center, and there was certainly nothing about the center itself or Molly and her assistant to worry Susan. Still, except for school, this was the first time Susan would be leaving Scott in the care of someone other than his grandmother for any longer than a few hours, and Susan was acutely conscious of the underlying reason for it to be happening now. So even though she was excited about her new job and eager to begin this new phase of her life, she couldn't help feeling sad about why these changes were taking place.

She knew that for a long time after Paul's death, Scott had felt abandoned. It had taken a lot of love and care on her part to make him understand that his father would never have willingly left him. Now she could only hope Scott didn't feel she was abandoning him, too.

She tried to shake off her concerns during the twenty-minute drive to the community college that was shared by two other towns within a half hour's driving distance of Rainbow's End. As she approached the sprawling, redbrick structure, which occupied several acres on the main highway leading south, she smiled in satisfaction. The school was lovely, she thought with pride, surrounded as it was by leafy oak trees and tall pines. Callahan Construction had built it, she remembered, as they had almost every important building in town. In fact, the company was the main reason Rainbow's End was home to the school rather than one of the other two towns, because Patrick Callahan had offered to build the school at cost, as long as it was located in Rainbow's End.

The mayors of the other two towns had grumbled a bit about "high-handed tactics" but neither had been willing to match Patrick's offer, which the mayor of Rainbow's End had pointed out with great pleasure.

Susan parked in the side lot and entered through the closest entrance, as she'd been instructed. From there, it was a short walk, down the corridor and to the right, to reach the administrative offices.

"Good morning, Susan."

Susan smiled at the plump brunette who stood behind a counter in the outer office area. "Good morning, Rhonda."

"You're sure early," Rhonda said. The big clock mounted on the wall showed the time to be five minutes after eight. Susan wasn't supposed to start until eight-thirty.

"You are, too," Susan pointed out.

Rhonda shrugged. "Yeah. I know. I like to get a jump on the day."

"Me, too."

"Well, come on in," Rhonda said, opening the swinging door that led to the inner sanctum. "I've got a bunch of stuff ready for you."

"Is Mr. Shaver in yet?" Susan inclined her head toward the closed door of her boss's office.

"Tom?" Rhonda grinned. "Nah, not him. He's never here early. In fact, it'll be a miracle if he can drag himself here by nine. He's totally unorganized, hon. That's why he needs us."

For the next ten minutes or so, Rhonda showed Susan around, gave her a set of keys and explained which doors they unlocked, and loaded her down with supplies.

Finally settled at her desk inside the president's suite of offices, Susan had just enough time to put her supplies away and pour herself a cup of coffee before the official eight-thirty start time.

However, just as Rhonda had predicted, Tom Shaver didn't arrive until ten after nine. A big, genial man with a ruddy complexion and thick salt-and-pepper hair, he gave Susan a welcoming smile and a hearty "Welcome" before entering his private office and indicating she should follow.

The morning was spent getting acquainted with her boss's routine and particular needs and idiosyncracies. He was adamant on only one score. "The name is Tom," he said when she called him Mr. Shaver. "It's okay to use 'Mr. Shaver' when students are in earshot or when you're talking to a parent or someone like that, but here, in my office, between us, it's Tom."

"Okay," Susan said, even though calling someone old enough to be her father by his first name was against her upbringing.

Susan ate lunch in the cafeteria, which was offering a limited menu during the summer. The food was fine, if nothing special.

"I told you," Rhonda said when Susan returned to the office. "I always bring my lunch."

"Tomorrow I will."

The afternoon was spent calling a list of suppliers and answering some of Tom's mountain of correspondence.

"I've gotten a bit behind," he said somewhat sheepishly.

Susan smothered a smile. Some of the letters were dated as far back as six weeks earlier. Yes, she could see why he needed an assistant.

"Actually, he needs a keeper," Rhonda said. But she smiled affectionately when she said it.

By the time five o'clock rolled around, Susan was tired, but it was a good tiredness, the kind that comes from the knowledge that you've done a good job and gotten a lot accomplished.

"So," Tom said, leaning back in his chair. "Your first day is over. Think you're going to like it here?"

Susan smiled and nodded happily. "Yes. I like it very much."

But as Susan drove back to town on her way to pick up Scott, her happiness and satisfaction dimmed as worries about how her son had fared today took their place.

She needn't have worried. Scott was happily working on a puzzle with three other kids and seemed almost reluctant to go home. Once they were in the car and on their way, he talked nonstop about everything he'd done that day and how nice Miss Molly was and what they were going to do tomorrow.

"And you know what, Mom? We're going to San Antonio to Sea World next week! I brought a permission slip home. It's okay for me to go, isn't it?"

It was with a profound sense of relief and thankfulness that Susan said of course Scott could go. And for the first time in a very long time, she felt almost lighthearted as she looked forward to the future.

Keith spent most of his first week at home doing odd jobs for his mother and hanging out with his brothers. On Saturday, Glenn, who was six years younger, came back from his vacation and he and Keith played catch-up.

But the whole time, in the back of his mind, were thoughts of Susan and Scott. He tried not to think of them—especially Susan—but his efforts were unsuccessful. On Monday, unable to resist, he drove by their house. He had no plan, just a vague idea that if he saw Scott outside, he'd stop. After all, he *had* promised the kid he'd come by again.

But the house looked closed up, as if they weren't home. Keith fought his disappointment, telling himself it was just as well. He had no business there, anyway.

Yet the following day, he drove by the house again. Still no activity. He slowed down, taking a good look. Everything looked quiet. Maybe they were away.

That evening, on impulse, he drove by again. And just as he drew even with the house, he saw Susan and Scott getting out of her Saturn. Before he could change his mind, he pulled into the driveway.

Scott's face lit up when he saw Keith's truck. He said something to his mother, and Susan turned around. Her smile was slower in coming.

Keith climbed out of his truck.

"Keith!" Scott called, running toward him. "Hi."

"Hi, Scott."

"Didya come to play basketball with me?"

By now Susan had walked toward them. She was all dressed up, Keith noticed, in a dark blue suit and pearls and heels. She looked beautiful, but a lot less approachable than that first day at Kroger when she wore shorts and a tank top. He wondered where she'd been.

"Hello, Keith," she said.

"Hi."

"I was just passing by and, uh, saw you, so—"

"He came to play basketball with me," Scott interjected eagerly. "Didn't you?"

"Yeah, I thought, if you weren't doing anything, we might shoot a few."

"Can I, Mom? Can I?"

After a brief hesitation, she smiled down at Scott. "All right. You can play while I get supper ready."

"Thanks, Mom! C'mon, Keith. Let's go."

Susan gave Keith another smile, then walked through the gate and disappeared from sight, although Keith could hear her unlocking the back door. He wished he had some reason to keep her outside, but he couldn't think of a thing. "Ready?" he said to Scott, who had dashed into the garage and emerged with the basketball.

For the next thirty minutes or so, they played a spirited game of one-on-one. Keith let Scott score a few points without being too obvious about it, and was rewarded with Scott's beaming smile.

"Let's take a break," Keith suggested when the heat finally began to get to them.

"Yeah," Scott said, panting. "I'm thirsty. Let's go get some water." He opened the gate, beckoning for Keith to follow.

Keith hesitated. As much as he wanted an excuse to see Susan again, he didn't feel right about barging into her house, even if Scott had invited him. But Scott had already gone into the back door, shouting, "Mom, we need something to drink!"

Still Keith hesitated. A few seconds later, Scott poked his head out. "Hey, aren't you comin', Keith? Mom has iced tea."

Keith started to say he'd drink his outside, but then he thought maybe he was making too big a deal out of this. There was no harm in going in for a glass of tea. Still, he wished Susan had been the one to invite him. He moved toward the door when she suddenly appeared in the doorway. There was a tall glass of iced tea in her hands. "Why don't you come in where it's cooler?" she said.

Keith smiled in relief. "Okay."

When he walked into the kitchen he saw that she was broiling chicken and that the table was already set for their dinner. She'd also changed her clothes and now wore a pair of denim shorts and a white T-shirt and sandals.

Keith leaned against the kitchen counter and drank his tea. He watched as Susan opened the refrigerator and removed store containers of potato salad and coleslaw.

"Now that I'm working, it's easier to buy some things ready-made," she said with an apologetic tone.

"Working?"

She nodded. "Yes. I started yesterday."

Keith didn't know why he was so surprised. Lots of women worked nowadays. In fact, most young women worked. But he thought Susan was a stay-at-home mom. In fact, he was sure she was. Then suddenly, it struck him. She'd *had* to go to work. Now that Paul was dead, she was the breadwinner. "Where are you working?"

She smiled. "For Tom Shaver, over at the community college. I'm his assistant.'' This last was said proudly. ''Do you know Tom?''

''I know who he is.''

''I'm going to Miss Molly's while Mom's at work,'' Scott piped up.

''Miss Molly's? You mean Molly Callahan's day-care center?''

''Yes,'' Susan said. ''It's a great place.''

It *was* a great place. Keith had stopped by there the other day, as a matter of fact, and been impressed with what his cousin's wife had done with the facility. ''Do you like your job?''

''So far I love it. It's going to take a while to get used to working, of course. I'm not very organized yet, but things will get better.''

Keith nodded slowly. She didn't seem to mind that she'd had to go to work. And Scott didn't seem to mind, either. But it bothered Keith that Susan probably hadn't had a choice. In a way, he was puzzled, too, because the Sheridan family certainly wasn't hurting for money.

He finished his tea, and even though he'd have liked to stay longer, he knew it was time to go. ''Guess I'll shove off. Thanks for the tea.''

''Scott, say goodbye to Keith, then go wash your hands,'' Susan said.

''Okay. And Mom? After we eat, can I go over to Ryan's house?''

Susan sighed. ''Scott…''

''Please?''

''You've been spending an awful lot of time over there. Maybe Mrs. DeAngelo is tired of—''

"She's not tired of having me." Scott turned to Keith. "My friend Ryan, his dad built him a tree house. Boy, you should see it. It's so neat."

"Why don't you ask Ryan if he wants to come over here tonight instead? You can swim."

Scott's face fell. "Aw, Mom. We like to play in the tree house. We have a club."

Keith smothered a smile. He remembered when he and Paul had had a "club," too. "So what's your friend's tree house like?"

Scott eagerly began describing the structure, ending with, "And his dad built a ladder to go with it, and everything." With his sneaker, he made circles on the floor. "I'll bet if my dad hadn't've died, he'd've built me a tree house, too."

Keith glanced at Susan. She looked stricken. "You know what?" he said impulsively. "I could build you one. In fact, you could help me."

Susan looked at Keith. She started to say something, then stopped. Her gaze moved to Scott, whose eyes were shining.

"I *could?* You *would?*" he squealed. "Mom? Isn't that *great?*"

"Yes," she said faintly. "That's great."

"When can we start?" Scott said.

"Well," Keith said, "I'll have to get the materials. I can do that tomorrow."

"We'll pay for the materials," Susan said.

"You don't have to do that. This was my idea."

"I insist. In fact, it's the only way I'm going to let you do this."

Keith could see from the expression on her face

that she meant what she said. "Okay," he said with a sigh. "You can pay for the materials."

"So can we start tomorrow night when I get home?" Scott said.

Keith smiled. "Sure." He looked at Susan. "What time?"

"We should be here by five-thirty," she said.

"I'll see you then."

After Keith left, Susan wondered what she could have done to prevent this development. Nothing, she guessed. Once Keith made the offer to build the tree house, she'd been trapped, because there was no way she was going to be responsible for extinguishing the shining happiness in her son's eyes.

But it was going to be tough having Keith around every night. Still, they'd be working outside, and she could stay indoors. That was it, she decided. She would greet Keith when he arrived, then make herself scarce. She hardly had to see him at all.

And before she knew it, the tree house would be finished and Keith would be going back to Alaska.

There's not a thing to worry about, she told herself firmly.

The following day, thoughts of Keith kept intruding at odd moments. By the time she picked up Scott at day care and they were on their way home, Susan knew she'd been lying to herself yesterday. There was plenty to worry about with Keith. She was far too attracted to him, and every time she saw him, she was reminded of the one thing she knew it was dangerous to dwell on: Scott's parentage. She knew it was silly, but she couldn't get rid of the notion that Keith might somehow divine her thoughts. Thank goodness he would only be in Rainbow's End a short time.

He was waiting for them when they arrived at the house. He waved as they passed his truck, which was parked in front, then backed into the driveway after them. The bed of the truck was filled with lumber and other materials.

"Hi," he said.

That smile of his had been her undoing once. Susan steeled herself as she walked toward him and tried to ignore the fluttering in her stomach. "Hi."

"Well, Scott, you ready?" Keith said.

"Yeah!"

"Before you start helping Keith, you need to change your clothes," Susan said. Once Scott was out of earshot, she looked at Keith. "This is awfully nice of you."

"It's my pleasure."

"I hate that you're tying up every afternoon, though."

"I don't mind a bit. It'll be fun."

"Yes, but you must have other things you want to do. After all, you only have a short time before you'll have to go back to Alaska."

"Yeah, well…"

Just the way he said the words caused alarm bells to go off in Susan's mind.

"Thing is, I've been thinking," he added, "maybe I won't go back."

"Oh?" she said weakly.

"Yeah, my dad really wants me to stay and work for the company, and..." He shrugged, his gaze meeting hers. "I don't know. I guess I didn't realize it, but I've really missed Rainbow's End."

Susan's heart was beating too fast. Dear God, she thought. This can't be happening. Keith can't really be planning to stay in Rainbow's End. Fear rendered her nearly speechless, and yet she knew she had to say something. "I—I thought you loved your work in Alaska."

"I do, but you know how it is. You get older. You start to think about what's important and what isn't."

She nodded. Swallowed.

"Truth is, I've missed my family."

Family. Dear Heaven. Scott. Laverne. And Scott's memories of Paul. All jeopardized now. "S-scott will be thrilled." She could have kicked herself for stammering. The last thing she wanted was for Keith to know how his news had thrown her. She was saved from having to say anything else by Scott's exuberant reappearance.

Promising to bring them something cold to drink, she made her escape. Once she reached the safety of the house, she covered her too-hot face with hands that trembled.

What was she going to do?

How was she going to keep Keith away, now that he and Scott had developed this bond? What excuse could she give that Scott would accept?

There was none.

Face it, she thought. Somehow you're going to have to let Keith remain in Scott's life without letting him disrupt *your* life. And, more importantly, without letting him know how you feel about him.

Chapter Eight

Although Keith's original motive for hanging around Susan's house was Susan herself, now he was as drawn to Scott as he was to the boy's mother. There was just something so great about the kid.

Thing is, he was so smart and so interested in everything. In addition, he was well-mannered and had a good sense of humor. Teaching him about carpentry had been a real pleasure and took Keith back to the days his father had taught *him* how to build things.

The boy was exactly the son Keith would have wished to have if he'd had kids of his own.

On the day the tree house was finally finished—exactly one week to the day after they'd begun building it—Keith knew he was going to really miss seeing Scott every day.

He couldn't help thinking about what it would be like to be a permanent part of Susan and Scott's life. And once the thought took root, there was no getting rid of it. After all, Susan was a widow. A young widow. She'd be bound to marry again someday, so why couldn't Keith be a candidate? The idea wasn't that far-fetched, was it?

Sure, ten years ago, it would have been impossible, but the situation today was nothing like it had been before. Paul was gone, and no amount of wishing otherwise would change that fact. So once a decent interval had passed, there was no reason Keith couldn't openly court Susan, was there?

Maybe Keith didn't have a chance, but he'd never know unless he tried. And if he *did* have a chance with her...well, wouldn't that be the best possible way to make up to Paul for what he'd done to him all those years ago? Wouldn't taking care of Paul's family, being a father to Scott, be the way to atone?

So when the last nail was driven into the tree house, and Keith and Scott had high-fived and inspected the finished structure with great mutual satisfaction, Keith said, "We have to celebrate."

"Yeah!" Scott said.

"Let's go call your mom and see if she wants to go out for pizza or something."

"But I've already got dinner started," Susan said when Keith told her what they wanted to do.

"Aw, Mom..." Scott said. "It's a celebration!"

She looked at the casserole she'd been about to put into the oven. "Well..."

"C'mon, Susan," Keith said. "The casserole will keep."

She bit her lip. "I guess I *could* save this for tomorrow night."

"All *right*," Scott said.

"But you're filthy. You can't go anywhere looking like that."

Keith grinned. Scott had dirt everywhere, including his clothes. Of course, Keith didn't look much better. "Tell you what," he said. "I'll go home and get cleaned up and while I'm gone, Scott can get cleaned up. I'll be back to get you two in an hour." He could tell Susan was still hesitant, but he didn't intend to give her an out.

She looked at Scott again. Sighed. Finally said a reluctant, "Okay."

Keith left before she could find another objection. He whistled all the way home.

Just how did she get roped into these things? Susan wondered as she changed into a nicer shorts outfit. *Oh, quit pretending you don't want to go. You wanted to say yes the moment Keith made the suggestion. You have zero willpower when it comes to Keith. It's been that way from the day you met him.*

Susan plopped down onto the side of her bed. Suddenly she was frightened. This situation with Keith was impossible. Yes, she was mightily attracted to him. And yes, she liked being with him. She liked being with him a lot. And under normal circumstances, she would be flattered and happy that he seemed to feel the same way.

But these weren't normal circumstances. And, as far as Keith was concerned, they never would be. The undeniable fact was, Keith was Scott's birth father. And there was no way she could have a relationship with him without telling him the truth. And that could *never* happen.

Once more, she ran through all the reasons in her head. First and foremost, there was Scott and his feelings about Paul. How could she ever tell him the man he'd adored was not his father at all? And secondly, there was Laverne. Even if Susan could eventually tell Scott the truth, learning that she was not the boy's grandmother would destroy Laverne.

Impossible. Completely impossible.

So what on earth was she doing?

Being with Keith was playing with fire. Tempting fate. Being dangerously stupid. All those things.

Oh, God. If only he had stayed in Alaska. If only he were going *back* to Alaska.

Well, he wasn't. He was going to be there in Rainbow's End where she would simply have to learn to deal with it.

Sighing, she got up and finished dressing.

"You sure look happy tonight."

Keith grinned at his mother, who was stirring a pot of stew. "I'm feeling good because we finished the tree house today, and it looks great."

His mother set her spoon down and wiped her hands on her apron. She looked at him thoughtfully. "I know you, Keith. It's more than that, isn't it?"

Keith hesitated, but only for a moment. Truth was,

he *wanted* to confide in someone. And who safer than his mother? "Maybe." He smiled self-consciously. "All right. Yeah, it *is* more than that. I really like being with Scott and Susan."

She smiled happily. "That's what I thought. Well, honey..." Walking over to him, she gave him a hug. "God bless you. I hope it works out."

"Then you approve?"

"What's not to approve of? Susan's a lovely girl, and Scott's a dear." Her expression turned serious again. "Does Susan feel the same way?"

"I don't know. It's too soon to say anything to her. I mean, Paul hasn't been gone that long."

"I'm glad you realize that. It's important not to rush her."

He nodded. "Listen, Mom, don't say anything to anyone else, okay? You're the only one who knows about this."

"What do you take me for? A blabbermouth?" she said with mock injury. "Besides, I don't want to jinx you. I'm having a hard enough time getting you boys married off."

Keith laughed. They said goodbye and Keith left. As he drove back to Susan's, he thought about his mother's admonition not to rush Susan. He knew she was right. And yet, if he were ever to have a chance with Susan, he knew he would have to talk to her about what had happened between them all those years ago. They couldn't just pretend it *hadn't* happened, the way they'd been doing.

Sooner or later, the truth had to be faced.

Suddenly, Keith made a decision. Never one to put

something off just because it was hard, he made up his mind that it would be better to face it and get it behind them. He would talk to her tonight.

The first person Susan saw when they entered the pizza place was Emma Tucker, who just happened to be the biggest gossip in Rainbow's End, as well as Laverne's next-door-neighbor.

"Susan!" Emma said, "It's so good to *see* you." Her curious eyes moved to Keith, giving him a thorough once-over.

Susan's heart sank. Tomorrow everyone in Rainbow's End would know Susan and Scott had been out with Keith. Tongues would wag and speculation would run high. A situation that was already difficult and complicated would become even more difficult and complicated.

Because she couldn't avoid it, Susan introduced Keith and Emma.

"Oh," Emma said, "*you're* the prodigal son that I've been hearing about. Welcome home."

Keith laughed. "I guess I am a bit of a black sheep, at least according to my father, who can't understand why anyone would ever want to leave Rainbow's End."

"How long are you staying?"

"I think I'm back for good."

"Well, that's good news! We can never have enough handsome, eligible bachelors around, can we, Susan?" Emma's glance was coy and knowing as it slid toward her.

Susan shifted uncomfortably. "That's true," she managed to say lightly.

"Mom, I'm hungry," Scott announced.

Thank God for small favors and small boys, Susan thought as they said goodbye to Emma and headed toward a booth at the other end of the restaurant. A few minutes later, she was relieved to see Emma and her husband leaving. She could feel herself relaxing once she was no longer the object of Emma's scrutiny.

After ordering their pizza, half with pepperoni to please Scott and half with mushrooms and black olives to please Susan—Keith said he would eat some of both—Scott asked if he could go play video games in the other room where the ringing and clanging of machines was in full throttle.

"Just until the pizza is ready," Susan said, who didn't approve of the games, with their concentration on violence and destruction.

Keith insisted on giving Scott money for the machines. "This is my treat tonight."

"We should be treating you." But Susan's protest was half-hearted, because her mind was still on Emma and the trouble the chance meeting might precipitate. What if she said something to Laverne? Chances are she would. In fact, it wouldn't have surprised Susan if she called Laverne the minute she got home. Normally, Susan wouldn't have cared in the least, but considering the way Laverne had acted that day Keith had had dinner with them, Susan couldn't help wishing that just this once Emma would keep her mouth shut.

Scott dashed off happily. Once he was gone, Keith leaned back in the booth. He studied her thoughtfully. "Thanks for coming tonight, Susan. I know you didn't want to."

Susan could feel herself blushing. She was grateful the lights were dim in this part of the restaurant. "What do you mean?"

His eyes held hers for a long moment. "Look," he finally said, leaning forward again, "since I've been back, we've been pretending nothing ever happened between us, but we both know something did. Don't you think it's time we talked about it?"

Susan's heart was beating so hard she was sure Keith could hear it. "I..." she began, then couldn't think what to say.

Keith reached across the table and laid his hand over hers. She swallowed. For long seconds, they simply looked into each other's eyes. Then, so softly she had to lean forward to hear him, he said, "I hope you've forgiven me for the way I treated you, Susan."

"Th-there's nothing to forgive," she said, finally finding her voice. "We were kids. We made a mistake."

"That's no excuse. I shouldn't have run out on you that way. I want you to know that I've always regretted it."

Slowly, she nodded.

"Did you ever tell Paul?"

"Tell Paul? Oh, my God, no! I could never have told him. He..." She took a deep breath, pulling her hand away in the process. "It would have caused him such needless pain.'' She shook her head. ''I couldn't do that.'' And then, even though it was one of the hardest things she'd ever done, she made a deprecating gesture. ''Why hurt him that way when what we did, it didn't mean anything, not really. It…it was just sex.''

He frowned, and for a moment, she thought he was going to contradict her. But just as quickly, the frown disappeared, and he nodded in agreement. ''You're right. I'm glad you didn't tell him. At least I don't have to have that on my conscience, too.''

''He…he did wonder why you left Rainbow's End so abruptly. I always wondered if the reason had to do with me and…and what happened between us.''

''That was part of it.''

He started to say more, but just then their number was called. ''I guess our pizza's ready.''

''Yes.''

''I'd better get it.''

She nodded.

''I'm glad we talked, though.''

''Yes. Me, too.''

He slid out of the booth.

''While you get the pizza, I'll get Scott,'' she said.

For the rest of the time they were in the restaurant, they kept the conversation casual and light, talking mostly about Susan's job and Keith's unsuccessful hunt for a place to live.

''Glenn's offered to share his apartment with me. Glenn's my younger brother,'' he explained.

''Yes, I remember.''

He shrugged. "I've gotten spoiled living on my own, though."

"I would have thought it would be fairly easy to find an apartment. There are a lot of new ones that have been built over the past year."

"Yeah, I know. Callahan Construction has built most of them. But I don't want an apartment. I'm looking for a small house."

"No wonder you're having a problem. Houses to rent are almost impossible to find."

"Tell me about it."

"What about a town house? There are some really nice ones over on the south end of town, near the college. I pass them every day on my way to work, and I've often thought, if I were single, that's where I'd live."

"You *are* single."

"Well, yes," she said, flustered. "But...oh, you know what I mean."

His smile was gentle. "Yes, I know what you mean."

"Anyway, those town houses are really nice."

"Actually, I'm considering them. Sheila lives over there."

"Your sister?"

"Yes. Do you know her?"

"I know who she is. She's gorgeous."

"Yeah. Kind of surprised me to see just *how* gorgeous. I can't believe she's not married yet."

"Girls don't get married quite so young nowadays."

"*You* got married young."

"Yes, but—" Appalled, she broke off. She'd almost said, *yes, but I had a reason.*

"But what?"

"But I was pretty mature for my age." Too late she realized she'd offered their youth as an excuse for what had happened between them ten years ago.

He didn't seem to notice the contradiction, though, answering, "Yeah, taking care of your mother and all, you had to grow up faster than most."

Susan put her hands in her lap to cover the fact that they were shaking from her nearly fatal slip of the tongue. She was going to have to be extra careful from now on, she realized, on her guard at all times.

Thank goodness they were nearly through with their pizza. After that near catastrophe, Susan wanted nothing more than to escape to the safety of her home.

The three of them were quiet on the short drive home—Keith and Susan lost in their own thoughts, and Scott finally tired out. When they reached Susan's house, Keith cut the ignition.

"You don't have to get out," Susan said when he reached for his door handle.

"I'll just make sure you get inside safely."

He walked them to the back door and waited until she'd unlocked it and turned on the light.

"Tonight was fun," Susan said. "Thanks for asking us."

"Yeah," Scott echoed. "Thanks, Keith."

Keith ruffled Scott's hair, but his eyes were on Susan. "It was my pleasure."

"Well, good night, then," Susan said.

"G-night," Scott said.

"Good night." He seemed about to say something else, then just raised his hand in farewell.

As she watched him walk through the gate, Susan wondered if she'd see him again. And even though she knew it would be best for everyone concerned if she didn't, she couldn't help hoping she would.

Susan wasn't surprised when her mother-in-law called her the following evening. After a few minutes of casual chitchat, Laverne said, "Emma Tucker told me she saw you and Scott at the pizza parlor last night."

"Yes."

"With Keith Callahan."

"Yes, with Keith."

For a long moment, there was silence. Then, in a strained voice, Laverne said, "You know, Susan, Paul has only been dead a little over eight months. It's really much too soon for you to be seeing other men."

Stung by the criticism, Susan's own voice was stiff when she answered. "I'm not *seeing* Keith, Mom. He's just a friend. Last night wasn't a date. He simply invited us to have pizza because he and Scott were celebrating the completion of the tree house."

"What tree house?"

Too late, Susan realized she hadn't told Laverne about the project. She'd meant to, but when she'd called her the other day, Laverne hadn't been home, and then Susan had gotten busy and forgotten to call again. Taking a deep breath, she explained.

"I see," Laverne said when Susan finished.

"I think it's very nice of him to take an interest in Scott." She knew she sounded defensive, but she couldn't help it. Laverne's attitude was hurtful. It was one thing for Laverne not to care for Keith, quite another to insinuate that Susan had done something wrong by being seen with him.

Silence reigned for long moments. Then Laverne sighed, the sound carrying clearly over the wire. And when she spoke, her tone was apologetic. "Susan, dear, I'm sorry. What I said before…it was out of line, but…but it just hurt me to think of you out with s-someone else." Her voice broke.

All Susan's anger evaporated. Pity and love softened her voice. "It's okay, Mom. I understand how you feel, and I'm not mad. But really, there's nothing for you to be concerned about, because Keith and I…we really are just friends."

After they hung up, Susan wondered if Laverne was going to be this way from now on. What if Susan *did* start dating? Was Laverne going to find fault with any man she might see? Or was it just Keith she objected to?

Susan sighed. Why did life have to be so complicated?

You could uncomplicate this situation easily. Just stop seeing Keith. You already know the relationship can't go anywhere, so why upset Laverne?

When she came right down to it, Laverne's call had given Susan the perfect out. The next time Keith suggested they do something together, Susan could tell him the truth—that it bothered Laverne to see him with Susan and Scott—and that Laverne's feelings were important to her, so it would be best all round if they stopped seeing each other.

But the thought of not seeing Keith anymore hurt. Wasn't it enough of a penance that she could never be with him in the way she wanted to, and that she could never acknowledge him as the father of her child? Surely there was no harm in being his friend and in allowing Scott to have Keith in his life.

Was there?

Keith signed the lease on one of the town houses in the same complex where Sheila lived the Saturday after the night he'd taken Susan and Scott out for pizza. He was anxious to move in, and even though the lease didn't start until the first of September, which was Tuesday, the manager said he could move in anytime.

So after finalizing the deal and paying his deposit and first month's rent, Keith drove to Austin and headed for one of the big furniture stores. In short order, he bought a couch, a coffee table, a recliner, a lamp, a bed and dresser, and a kitchen table and chairs. The store promised delivery first thing Monday.

Pleased with his day's work, he drove back to Rainbow's End, arriving home at five-thirty.

"Oh, good," his mother said when he walked in. "You're home in time to go with us."

"Go with you where?"

"The men's club at church is having their annual

spaghetti supper and auction tonight. We're all going. Unless you have plans?''

"No, no plans. Are you leaving now?"

"Pretty soon."

Why not? He didn't have anything better to do tonight. He *had* flirted with the idea of calling Susan. But it was really too late in the day for that. Maybe he'd give her a call tomorrow. "Okay. I'll go. Just let me wash up a little first.''

Holy Family was the parish where Keith's parents had been married and he and his siblings had been baptized and made their first holy communion and confirmation. Walking into the parish hall where the spaghetti supper and auction were being held was like old home week, because Keith knew most of the people there.

"There's Patrick and Jan and the kids,'' Rose said, pointing to a long table on the far side of the room. She started in their direction, followed by Keith and his father.

"Keith!''

Keith turned at the sound of his name. A beaming Scott was heading in his direction, followed more slowly by Susan. Keith felt a quick leap of pleasure, which he didn't try to hide. "Hey, sport,'' he said, giving Scott's shoulder a quick squeeze. "Good to see you. How's the tree house holding up?"

"It's great!'' Scott said. "My friends think it's really cool. Hey, Mom. Look. It's Keith.''

"Yes, I see.'' Susan smiled at Keith. "Hi.'' Looking beyond Keith, she said, "Hello, Mrs. Callahan. Mr. Callahan.''

"Susan, how nice to see you," Rose said. "Are you here by yourself?"

"Uh-huh."

"In that case, we'd love to have you sit with us."

"Oh, no, I don't want—"

"Now I'm not going to take no for an answer," Rose said. Her eyes met Keith's briefly.

"Well," Susan said. "If you really want us…"

"This will give us an opportunity to get caught up," Rose said, putting her arm around Susan's shoulders.

Things couldn't have worked out better if he'd planned them, Keith thought as they all headed toward the table where several of his brothers were already seated. Maybe fate was trying to tell him something.

Chapter Nine

Maybe it was fate, Susan thought, that she and Keith seemed to constantly be thrown together. Although, if she'd been thinking when she decided to bring Scott tonight, she would have realized the Callahans were bound to be there in full force. After all, Holy Family was their parish, and if Susan wasn't mistaken, she'd read something in the *Rainbow's End Register* about Keith's father being a newly elected member of the parish council.

Or maybe, she thought wryly, her subconscious had purposely steered her in this direction. She watched as Keith greeted the rest of his family. What was wrong with her, that just the sight of him caused her resolve to melt as if it had never existed?

"Hi, Susan."

Susan turned and smiled at Jan Callahan, Patrick's wife. She and Jan had served together on the elementary-school PTA board the previous year, and Susan had enjoyed getting to know the other woman. "Hi, Jan," she said with pleasure. "It's good to see you again."

"You, too. Are you going to sit with us?"

Susan nodded. "Your mother-in-law invited me to."

"Oh, good. I've missed talking to you." Jan's gaze moved to Scott. "Hi, Scott."

"Hello, Mrs. Callahan," Scott said politely.

Briana, Jan's nine-year-old, who was in Scott's class in school, gave him a shy wave from the other side of the table. Scott, who wasn't shy at all, walked over to talk to her. Susan smothered a smile as she saw the telltale pink that colored Briana's cheeks. We females are all alike, Susan thought, whether we're nine or ninety. We get a little attention from an attractive male and we turn to mush. Unable to resist, she glanced at Keith again. He looked terrific tonight, dressed in casual khaki Dockers and a navy cotton shirt open at the throat. Her pulse picked up speed just looking at him. Unexpectedly, he turned, and Susan hurriedly looked away. She knew her cheeks were probably as pink as little Briana's, and she could have kicked herself for letting him catch her observing him.

"Sit down by me." Jan patted the chair next to her.

"All right."

"I hear you've gone to work for Tom Shaver,"

Jan said once Susan was settled. "How do you like it?"

"I love it."

"Tom's an awfully nice guy," Jan said.

"Yes, he is."

"So what are you doing there?"

While Susan was telling Jan about her job, Rose sat across the table from Susan. A few minutes later Keith walked over and took the seat next to his mother. Within seconds Scott, still in the throes of hero-worship, plopped down next to Keith. Although Susan wasn't looking at him—she certainly didn't want him catching her *again*—she could feel Keith watching her. Immediately, she felt unsettled.

What is wrong with me? she thought angrily. *I am a grown woman. Why does Keith's mere presence have the ability to make me come unglued?* Determined not to let him see, by so much as a flicker of her eyes, how he affected her, she kept her attention firmly fixed on Jan.

"Your job sounds great," Jan said wistfully when Susan finished describing it. She leaned closer, lowering her voice. "I'm thinking of going to work, too."

"Are you?"

"You *are?*" This was from Rose.

Jan looked at her mother-in-law. "You weren't supposed to hear that, Mom."

"Why not? Did you think I wouldn't approve?"

"I *knew* you wouldn't approve."

Rose shrugged. "Well, I know I'm old-fashioned,

but I do think mothers should be home when their children are little.''

''Allene's going to be in school all day this year,'' Jan pointed out.

''I know.''

''And if I need after-school care, I couldn't find anyone better than Molly to watch her and Briana.''

''That's true.'' But Rose's tone of voice very clearly said she wasn't convinced.

''Anyway, I wasn't thinking of a full-time job,'' Jan said. ''Maybe just four or five hours a day. Or even a couple of days a week.''

''Hey, Jan,'' Sheila said from farther down the table, ''it's *your* life. If you want to get a job, I say go for it.''

''You would,'' Rory said.

''Mind your own business,'' Sheila said.

''You're not minding *yours*,'' Rory shot back.

Susan bit back a smile. She was glad to see that Keith's family wasn't perfect. She was also glad to see that it wasn't just *her* mother-in-law who thought a mother's place was in the home.

While this conversation was taking place, two of the servers—members of the C.Y.O.—had started placing steaming plates of spaghetti and meatballs in front of each of them. Another server carried a tray of drinks and still another was distributing baskets of garlic bread. Each place already had napkin-wrapped utensils and in the middle of the table were shakers of parmesan cheese and salt and pepper.

''Sheila's right,'' Rose said. ''If you want to go to work, it's your business.''

Sheila grinned. "Gee, thanks, Ma." Her gray eyes turned to Jan again. "Word of advice, Jan. Just don't ask to work on the construction crew!"

"Jeez, Sheila," Patrick Jr. said. "Give it a rest." Addressing Susan, he said, "She's the stubbornest person I've ever known."

"Oh, really? That's the pot calling the kettle black!"

Keith laughed. "You can say that again."

"Hey," Sheila said, leaning forward to see him. "You're skating on thin ice, you know, so maybe you should be quiet."

"What do you mean, *I'm* skating on thin ice?"

"Just what I said."

"What's she talking about?" Keith said.

His father sighed. "She's mad because you've been away all these years, but the minute you're back, you have a job with the company."

"Whereas *I've* been old faithful," Sheila said, "and Dad doesn't care."

"Sheila," Patrick Sr. said in a warning tone. "Enough is enough. We've been over this ground before."

Sheila exchanged a look with Jan. "And we'll be over it again," she grumbled, but softly.

Her father ignored her. "Would you please pass the bread?" he said to Susan.

Susan smiled and handed him the basket. She was fascinated by the way Keith's family related to one another. It was obvious they had plenty of disagreements, yet they didn't let those disagreements change the way they felt about each other. A familiar pang of envy pierced her. It would be so nice to belong to a large and loving family like this one. She wondered if they realized how lucky they all were to have each other.

"So Susan," Rose said cheerily, "how is your mother-in-law doing?"

"Much better, thank you."

"I'm so glad. I know these past months must have been awfully hard for her."

"Yes, they have."

Rose's expression softened. "It's been hard for you, too," she said gently.

Susan nodded. Out of the corner of her eye she could see that Keith and Scott were busy talking, and she was glad. Rose seemed to understand that Susan really didn't want to talk about the loss of Paul, especially not now, with Scott so near, and she dropped the subject.

For the remainder of the meal, the talk was light and impersonal, and by the time they'd finished eating, Susan felt more relaxed than she'd felt in a long time. The Callahans were all such nice people, she thought. So genuine and kind, and so easy to be around.

And then she finally acknowledged the other thought. The one that was lodged in the back of her mind. The one that refused to go away. The one that went, *what if I'd married Keith instead of Paul?*

Immediately she felt so disloyal. Paul had been a wonderful husband. A wonderful father. She should be ashamed of herself for even *thinking* anything else. Once again she made a determined effort to clear her mind, to think only of the present.

By now the helpers were starting to clear the tables. In short order, the job was done, and the men's club members began setting out the items that would be auctioned off. Scott and Briana raced off to look at everything. Susan and Jan followed more slowly.

"Mom, Mom!" Scott called. "Come over here and see this!"

"Uh-oh," Jan said. "Now you're in trouble."

When Susan reached the table where he stood, she saw what had put that excited sparkle into his eyes. It was a beautiful collection of about a dozen antique wooden cars. They were hand painted in intricate detail, and the workmanship was flawless.

"Aren't they cool?" Scott said in awe. He prodded one of the cars with his forefinger. Smoothly, it moved a couple of inches.

"Yes, they're very nice." Gently, she added, "Honey, I know you like them, but I'm afraid they're too expensive for me to bid on."

"I know, Mom. I just wanted you to see them 'cause they're so cool."

Susan's heart swelled with pride at this evidence of maturity on his part. A lot of kids his age would whine and pout if told they couldn't have something they wanted, but Scott wasn't like that. Oh, he did his share of pressing his case, especially when it came to going places or doing things his friends were doing, but he wasn't greedy, nor was he selfish. And because he didn't whine, she suddenly wished she *could* afford the cars. After all, she could save them and give them to him at Christmas.

When they got back to the table, Scott eagerly told Keith about the cars.

"I'd like to see those," Keith said.

There was a lump in Susan's throat as she watched father and son walk off together. It amazed her that no one else could see how alike they were, when to her eyes, it was impossible *not* to see.

"Keith is so good with kids," Jan said.

"Yes," Rose agreed. "He needs to get married and have some of his own."

Susan's heart thumped foolishly. She wondered if Rose had said that with some ulterior motive, but no, when she looked at Rose, she was positive Rose's comment had been innocently made.

"Oh, Mom," Jan said, laughing. "You say that about all your sons."

"Yes, because it's *true* of all my sons. But it's particularly true of Keith, I think."

"Why do you say that?" Jan said curiously.

"I can't explain it. Mothers just know these things."

Susan shifted uncomfortably. She wished they would talk about something else.

Just then, in answer to her wish, the auctioneer walked up onto the stage and began testing the microphone.

"Okay, folks," he said a few minutes later. "Take one last good look at the items you want, then take your seats and we'll begin the auction."

A few minutes later Keith and Scott came back to

the table, and five minutes later, the auction started. The most inexpensive items were auctioned first. Susan hadn't intended to bid on anything, but about halfway through the auction, when a particularly lovely crocheted tablecloth was up for bids, she couldn't help thinking what a nice Christmas present it would make for Laverne. She joined in the spirited bidding, and to her amazement, got the tablecloth for eighty dollars.

"Way to go, Susan!" said Jan.

"Yeah, Susan," said Sheila.

"Good for you," said Rose, amid a general chorus of congratulations.

Susan sat back, flushed and pleased with herself. Her adrenaline was still pumping after the excitement of the competition. Her gaze met Keith's, and he gave her a thumbs-up and a grin. His obvious approval, combined with the welcoming friendliness of his family throughout the evening, filled her with a warm glow of happiness.

A dozen items later, the antique cars came on the block. Susan gave Scott a commiserating smile when the bidding started at fifty dollars. Obviously, the cars would sell for at least several hundred.

"I have fifty. Do I hear seventy-five?" the auctioneer called in his singsong voice.

Suddenly, surprising everyone, Keith's hand shot up. "Seventy-five," he said.

What was he doing? Surely he wasn't bidding on the cars for Scott! Susan tried to catch his eye, but he was looking at the auctioneer.

After that, the bidding was fast-paced and heated.

In no time at all, it seemed to Susan, the bid was up to two hundred and fifty dollars and only Keith and another man were still bidding.

"Do I hear two-seventy-five?" the auctioneer said, looking first at Keith, then at the other man, who had made the last bid.

Keith pursed his lips. For a few moments there was silence as the audience, caught up in the competition, held its collective breath.

"Two fifty once. Two fifty twice," the auctioneer said.

"Three hundred!" Keith called out.

The audience gasped. Everyone looked at the other man who, after a long moment, finally shook his head, and the bidding was over. Amid cheers, a triumphant Keith walked up front to claim his prize. When he came back to the table ten minutes later, he had a large box in his arms. With a smile, he set it down in front of Scott. "Happy Birthday," he said.

Susan's mouth dropped open.

Scott, eyes nearly popping out of his head, looked up at Keith. "B-but it's not my birthday."

Keith grinned. "Maybe not today. But it will be one of these days, won't it?"

"Keith," Susan said, finally finding her voice. "He can't accept those."

Keith's eyes—so like Scott's—met hers. "Why not?"

"Because it…it's too much, that's why."

"Aw, come on, Susan. It's no big deal."

"But it *is* a big deal." Susan looked at Rose and Jan for support, but neither woman said anything.

Rose had an odd look on her face, though, and Susan was sure Keith's mother agreed with her but didn't want to oppose her son.

"Look at it this way," Keith said. "I've missed all Scott's birthdays, and as Paul's best friend, you know I would have given Scott something if I'd been here. So consider this a makeup present for all those years."

"I appreciate the sentiment, but I still think—"

"Besides," Keith said, "I'll probably want to play with these cars as much as Scott."

Susan looked at Scott. Naked longing was in his eyes.

"When *is* his birthday, anyway?" Keith said.

"D-December 20th," she stammered, knowing she was blushing.

"Well, shoot," Keith said. "In that case, it's a birthday present *and* a Christmas present. Now you really *can't* refuse, Susan."

"Man," Scott said in wonderment. "This is the best present I ever had. Thanks, Keith!"

Keith smiled happily. His gaze, meeting Susan's again, said *you wouldn't spoil this, would you?*

After a moment, Susan gave him a weak smile. "Thank you," she mouthed.

There were only a couple more items left to auction, and then it was time to go home. Susan said goodbye to everyone, leaving Keith for last.

"Thank you again," she said. "It was very generous of you to buy him the cars."

"I told you," Keith warned, "I plan to come and

play with them, too.'' His eyes were warm as they met hers.

''You're welcome anytime.'' She could hardly tear her gaze away and knew his eyes were following them as they left the hall.

As she and a thrilled Scott drove home, Susan told herself that under the circumstances, there was no other answer she could have given.

Keith's brothers began teasing him the minute Susan and Scott were out of earshot.

''*Now* we know the reason you decided to stay in Rainbow's End,'' Patrick Jr. said.

''Yeah, and her name is Susan,'' Rory said. He winked. ''Don't blame you, bro. She's a fox.''

Kevin elbowed Glenn. ''And here we thought he missed *us.*''

''Come on, you guys,'' Keith said, but it was hard to sound indignant. He avoided looking at his mother, afraid if he did, one or the other of them would give him away completely.

''Smart move,'' Rory said, ''buying the kid those cars. I've never known a woman yet who could resist a man that likes her kid.''

''That's not why I bought the cars.'' But maybe it was. Maybe he'd wanted to see that look in Susan's eyes as much as he'd wanted to please Scott.

In answer, Rory and the others only smiled at him.

''Come on, boys,'' Patrick Sr. said. ''I volunteered all of you to help with the cleanup.''

After they were finished, Glenn, Kevin and Rory said they were going to Pot O' Gold.

''Wanna come?'' Rory said, looking at Keith.

"No, I don't think so. It's been a long day, and I'm tired."

"You don't have to stay late."

"I know. I guess I'm just not in the mood."

"He wants to go home and dream about Susan," Kevin taunted.

Keith pretended to punch Kevin, and there was a good-natured scuffle.

Rory fell into step with Keith as they walked outside. "You *do* like her, don't you?" he said.

There was no sense pretending he didn't understand the question, so Keith answered honestly. "Yes."

Rory nodded. He didn't say anything for a long moment. Then, surprising Keith, he threw his arm around Keith's shoulder. "Go for it, then."

Much later, after Keith was in bed, he thought back over the evening. He couldn't remember when he'd had a more satisfying one. Having Susan and Scott there with his family, seeing how they fit in, then buying those cars for Scott and seeing the happiness in the kid's eyes...

Keith had felt like a million bucks.

And he was determined to hang on to that feeling. The last of his guilt over the past had finally disappeared.

Go for it, Rory had said.

He *would* go for it. From now on, he would do whatever it took to win Susan.

Cowardice and youthful stupidity had caused him to walk away from her once. He had no intention of doing it again. This time he intended to stick around for the duration, whether she wanted him to or not.

Chapter Ten

Susan spent all Sunday afternoon cleaning house, even though she would much rather have done something fun with Scott. Wiping sweat off her forehead, she thought longingly of the pool or a nice, air-conditioned movie. She sighed. Guess having fun on the weekends was a thing of the past. Now that she was working, the only time she had for housework was weekends.

She should have cleaned yesterday, but she'd had errands to run and bills to pay and a dozen other things that had taken up the day. Then, of course, they'd gone to the spaghetti dinner last night. And this morning, they'd gone to church.

Maybe she should try to find a cleaning service. She seemed to remember getting a coupon in the mail a week or so ago about a new service that was starting up in the area. She wondered how expensive one would be. Although Paul had had a decent amount of life insurance, it was earmarked for emergencies and Scott's education. Susan didn't want to have to dip into it unless it was absolutely necessary.

Her mind thus occupied, she finished up in the kitchen, which she'd saved for last, and took the bucket containing the water she'd used to mop the kitchen floor outside to dump it. She was rinsing the bucket under the outside faucet when she heard a car pull into the driveway. Putting the bucket down, she dried her hands against the sides of her denim shorts, then opened the gate and walked out.

Her mother-in-law was just getting out of her Buick. "Hi," she said. "I went into Austin for the day and thought I'd stop by for a few minutes before going home."

"I'm glad you did." Laverne looked good today, Susan thought, giving her a fond smile. The dark circles that had been under her eyes for months after Paul's death were mostly gone. Maybe she was finally starting to accept his loss. Susan hoped so. "Come on in. I was just about to have a glass of iced tea."

"That sounds wonderful. I'm parched."

"It's no wonder, with this heat. What were you doing in Austin? Shopping?"

"Yes."

They walked through the gate to the back door.

"Is Scott home?" Laverne asked.

"No, he went over to David Chandler's house, but

he should be home soon. I told him four o'clock. So where were you shopping?'' Susan held the screened door open.

''Oh, Foley's and Dillard's and a couple of other places. Everyone's having end-of-summer sales, so I picked up some good buys.'' She indicated the shopping bag in her hand. ''I got Scott a couple pairs of those nice denim shorts.''

They walked inside.

''Oh, good. He's about outgrown all the ones he had this year.''

Laverne smiled. ''I noticed.''

''Well, I'm glad you had fun today.'' Susan couldn't remember the last time she'd gone shopping. Not since before Paul's death.

''It *was* fun. I got some clothes to take to California, too. Oh, and I met Norma for lunch.'' Norma Ford was Laverne's best friend from college. She was a widow who lived in Georgetown, just north of Austin.

''That was nice. How is Norma?''

''She's doing great. She's started a new exercise program and she's lost about ten pounds. She looks terrific.'' While Laverne chattered on about Norma, Susan got out the pitcher of iced tea and poured them both a glass. ''I have some sugar cookies, too. Want some?''

Laverne shook her head. ''No, thanks. I had a big lunch.''

Susan sat down and they talked. A few minutes later she heard the back screen door open and bang shut. She smiled. ''Scott's home.''

Laverne's eyes lit up. She turned around to greet him.

Scott came barreling into the kitchen. "Hi, Gran."

"Hello, sweetheart." Laverne held her arms open, and after only a moment of hesitation, Scott submitted to her hug.

Susan made a mental note to speak to him about his recent reticence when it came to physical demonstrations of affection, especially in relation to his grandmother. She knew his behavior was normal. He'd reached an age where he considered hugging and kissing to be babyish, but Susan knew Laverne was terribly vulnerable right now and could easily be hurt. Scott was, at heart, sensitive and caring, and he loved his grandmother. If Susan explained how important it was that he not act as if he were rejecting her, he would understand.

"So what have you been doing all week?" Laverne said happily. She reached up and brushed Scott's hair back from his face. Her eyes shone with love.

He shrugged. "You know. Stuff."

"That's the trouble," she said in a mock serious voice. "I'm an old lady, and I don't know about *stuff*."

He grinned. "You're not old."

"Of course I am. But that's okay. I don't mind. Now come on, humor me. Tell me about your week."

While Scott talked, he walked over to the refrigerator and took out the orange juice. "And Wednesday we finished the tree house and went for pizza with Keith, and Thursday David came over, and yesterday me and Mom got my school supplies and then we went to the spaghetti dinner at—'' Abruptly, he stopped. ''Gran! I forgot! You haven't seen my cars!''

Susan, who had gotten up to get him a glass, froze. If she could have stopped him, she would have. Unfortunately, nothing short of an earthquake would stop him now, and she knew it.

''Cars?'' Laverne said, a quizzical smile on her face.

''Yeah! They're s-o-o-o-o cool. They're upstairs in my room. C'mon. I'll show you.'' He put the carton of juice on the table.

Giving Susan an indulgent smile, Laverne got up and followed Scott out of the room.

Susan used the time they were gone to collect her thoughts. What would Laverne think when she found out who had given the cars to Scott? There was no doubt she would know by the time she came downstairs again, because Scott would eagerly broadcast the information the moment she admired them. He thought the sun rose and set in Keith, and he would have no qualms over expressing his feelings to his grandmother.

Oh, God. Susan knew Laverne would be upset. If their going to have pizza with him had upset her, the gift of the antique cars would cause a major storm.

Sure enough, when the two of them returned to the kitchen ten minutes later, there was a tightening to Laverne's mouth that hadn't been there earlier.

''Gran thinks the cars are neat,'' Scott pronounced.

"Yes," Susan said weakly. She was angry with herself because she could hardly meet Laverne's eyes, and darn it, she had nothing to feel guilty about. She had done nothing wrong.

"Is this mine?" Scott picked up the glass of orange juice Susan had poured.

Susan nodded. Laverne sat back down at the table and picked up her half-full glass of iced tea. After a moment, Susan sat, too. Scott, oblivious to the undercurrents, sank into his chair, saying, "I'm hungry. Can I have some chips?"

"No chips, but you can have some cheese and crackers," Susan said, grateful for the diversion.

"Okay." He walked to the pantry and took out a box of crackers.

After a few more moments of silence, Laverne finally spoke. "Scott tells me Keith Callahan bought him those cars as an early birthday present."

The frostiness of her voice told Susan exactly what her mother-in-law was thinking. "Yes." Susan was angry with herself for feeling so guilty. She cleared her throat to gain some time. "I thought it was much too expensive a gift, however..." She went on to explain Keith's rationale about missing Scott's previous birthdays.

"Yes, well, I agree with you." Laverne eyed Scott, who was busily putting Cheez Whiz on Ritz crackers and didn't seem to be paying attention. Lowering her voice, she said, "How much did those cars cost?"

Susan answered as evenly as she could.

Laverne's eyes widened. "Susan..." she murmured. "That's outrageous. Completely unsuitable. Why, *I've* never even spent that much on a gift for Scott."

"I know, Mom, I know. But Keith insisted." She wished Laverne would drop the subject. It was not an appropriate one to talk about in front of Scott, although he was still engaged in fixing his snack and did not seem to be listening to their conversation. Still, you never knew with kids. He might just be pretending not to listen.

Laverne shook her head. Her gaze was thoughtful. "Tell me, just how did you happen to be at the auction with Keith, anyway?"

Although her mother-in-law's question was casual, Susan knew the question was anything but. Calling on all the willpower she possessed, she managed to keep her answer light. "We weren't *with* Keith. We just happened to bump into the Callahans, and Rose Callahan invited us to sit with the family."

"I see," Laverne said.

No, you don't see, Susan wanted to say. *You're thinking something that's not true.* And yet, wasn't there just a *grain* of truth to Laverne's suspicions? *Weren't you thrilled to be asked to sit with the Callahans? Didn't you enjoy every minute of it? And wasn't the biggest reason for your enjoyment the fact that you could be with Keith in a way that wasn't planned?*

I haven't done anything wrong, Susan reminded herself again, more angrily this time.

"How *is* Rose?" Laverne said. "I haven't seen her in ages."

"I know. She mentioned that."

By now Scott had finished making his snack and he returned to the table and began to eat. For the remainder of Laverne's visit, the subject of the cars and Keith was dropped, but several times Susan could tell from the expression in Laverne's eyes that she was thinking about it again. Susan wanted to explain further, but she knew she couldn't. The more she tried to defend herself, the more convinced Laverne would be that there really was something going on between Susan and Keith. It was best to let the subject drop.

At five o'clock Laverne stood. "It's getting late. I'd better be going. What are you two doing for dinner tonight?"

Susan shrugged. "I don't know. I hadn't thought about it. Why?"

"Well, I thought maybe you might like to go out somewhere? Maybe to Mama's?"

"Yeah!" Scott said, grinning. "Yeah, Mom, let's go!" Mama's was a small, family-owned Mexican restaurant and one of his favorites.

"All right," Susan said. They hadn't had Mexican food in at least two weeks. "That sounds good."

They decided on the time, and Susan said she and Scott would come by and pick up Laverne, who didn't like driving at night. Then after giving Scott a hug and kiss, Laverne left.

Before her car had even pulled out of the driveway, Scott said, "Mom, I've got an idea!"

"Oh? And what is that?"

"Why don't we call Keith and ask him to go to Mama's with us tonight?"

Susan was so taken aback by this suggestion, for a moment, she didn't answer. Finally she found her voice. "I don't think so, Scott."

Scott frowned. "Why not? Keith *really* likes Mexican food, and he's never been to Mama's."

"How do you know he's never been to Mama's?"

"He told me."

"He *told* you?"

"Yeah. When we were buildin' my tree house. We were talking, and Keith said he really missed Mexican food when he lived in Alaska, and I told him Mama's had the best Mexican food in town, 'cause that's what Dad always said, and Keith said he'd never been there." Scott said all this so fast, he was breathless by the time he finished.

"Well, I'm sorry, honey, but it wouldn't be right to ask Keith to come with us. Not when your grandmother invited us to have dinner with her."

Scott's frown deepened into a scowl. "But I want him to come," he said stubbornly.

The fact that Scott was normally a very well-behaved child was the reason Susan decided not to chide him for his unbecoming behavior right now. "Remember what I told you? That we don't necessarily get what we want all the time? Well, this is one of those times." Good grief, she could just imagine what Laverne would have to say if they were to show up with Keith in tow tonight!

"But why not? Don't you like Keith?"

"Whether or not I like Keith is not the point,

Scott. The point is that when someone invites you to do something, they're inviting *you*," Susan explained patiently. "They don't want you inviting other people to come along."

Scott opened his mouth, his expression saying he was going to protest.

"Now I don't want to hear another word about it, okay?" Susan said firmly.

Scott didn't look happy, and he muttered a bit under his breath, but he was smart enough to know when Susan meant business, so he didn't continue the argument.

Susan almost added, *and please don't talk about Keith tonight,* then thought better of it. Calling Scott's attention to the fact that Laverne didn't like Keith would only confuse the boy and raise questions Susan didn't feel equipped to answer.

Later, though, Susan was sorry she hadn't talked to Scott further, because they had no sooner sat down at their table at Mama's when Scott said, "I wanted Mom to call and invite Keith to come tonight, Gran, but she wouldn't. She said you wouldn't like it, but you wouldn't have cared, would you?"

Oh, my God, Susan thought. She knew her face was turning red. She could have strangled Scott.

Laverne's eyes briefly met Susan's before turning to Scott. "Well, honey, actually, your mother was right. I *would* have cared."

"But why? Keith's nice, and he was Dad's best friend! He's fun, too. I like him."

Susan knew what it must have cost Laverne to smile as affectionately as she did. "I'm sure he is fun, sweetheart, and I know you like him. But I'm awfully selfish when it comes to my two favorite people in the world. I don't like to share you with anyone else. You can understand that, can't you?''

Susan noticed that Laverne didn't say *I like him, too.*

Scott thought about what his grandmother had said for a moment. Then, giving her an embarrassed smile, he said, ''Yeah, Gran, I understand.''

Laverne reached across and squeezed Scott's hand. ''Good.''

Keith's name wasn't mentioned again, but Susan knew her mother-in-law hadn't forgotten about him, any more than Susan had. Susan also knew the subject was bound to come up again, because even though Susan didn't want to hurt Laverne, she also didn't want to give up seeing Keith. And if she continued seeing him, even just as a friend, Laverne was bound to hear about it, either through the well-oiled gossip network or through a remark of Scott's.

Even if Susan *wanted* to stop seeing Keith, Scott would never let her. His obstinance tonight when he'd wanted her to invite Keith to come along to dinner had shown her that.

Susan sighed.

Why was life so difficult?

''I really like Susan Sheridan, don't you?'' For a moment, Jan Callahan wasn't sure her husband had heard her, because he continued scouring the sink and didn't answer. It was Sunday evening, the day after the dinner at the church, and the two of them were just finishing cleaning up the kitchen after dinner.

Patrick finally turned around. "Yeah, I like Susan." He grinned. "What's on your mind?"

"What do you mean, what's on my mind?"

"Just what I said. I know you, Jan. You never ask idle questions. There's always a reason behind them."

Jan smiled sheepishly. "Okay, you're right. I just thought, seeing them together last night, that Keith and Susan are perfect for each other."

"Now Jan..."

"I know, I know, you hate matchmaking."

"With good reason."

Jan grimaced, remembering how her last attempt at bringing two people together had backfired, resulting in the near loss of two friends.

"Your trouble," her husband said, "is you're a romantic and you think everyone else feels the same way."

"No..." She walked over to him and put her arms around his waist. She gave him a soft smile. "My trouble is, I'm so happy with you, and I want everyone else to be happy, too."

Patrick, who always knew a cue when he heard one, lifted her face for a kiss. Jan sighed with pleasure and closed her eyes. She and Patrick had been married for sixteen years now, since Patrick was twenty-two and she was twenty-one, but the spark was still alive. One kiss led to another. Their breathing quickened and she could feel him hardening against her. His hands moved down to cup her bottom, and he pulled her tight against him.

"Let's go upstairs," he muttered.

Shaking her head regretfully, she said, "You know we can't. The kids are still awake."

"So? They're watching TV. They won't miss us." He laughed softly. "C'mon, hon, we'll have a quickie."

"Later," she whispered, kissing him hard, then pushing herself away. She gave him a teasing smile. "And it won't be a quickie!" She took a deep breath to slow her heartbeat. Amazing, she thought, how, within minutes, he could still turn her on.

"I'm not going to let you forget," he warned.

"As if I wanted to…"

They smiled at each other, then Patrick got back to the business of the unfinished sink.

A few minutes later, Jan said, "How about if we have a dinner party next weekend and invite Susan and Keith?"

Patrick laughed. "You're not going to forget about this, are you?"

"Nope."

He shrugged. "Go ahead. I don't care. Just don't make it too obvious, okay?"

"I won't. I'll ask Jackie and Alan, too, and maybe Sophie and Tucker." The other two couples were longtime friends.

"Fine. Whatever you want. But Jan…"

"What?"

"Don't get too carried away with this, okay? I mean, having them for dinner is fine, but after that, it's gotta be hands-off. Whatever happens next, if anything *does* happen, will be up to them. Agreed?''

"Agreed."

Undaunted by her husband's cautionary words, Jan smiled happily. Everything was going to work out great, she was sure of it, especially with a little judicious help from her. By the time she and Patrick had finished up in the kitchen and joined their daughters in the family room, she was already spinning daydreams about being asked to be the matron of honor at Susan and Keith's wedding and then, how afterwards she and Patrick would be the godparents for their first child.

Tomorrow, she decided, she would call Susan and get the ball rolling.

"Call for you on line two, Susan."

"Thanks, Rhonda."

Susan punched the indicated line. "Susan Sheridan."

"Susan? Hi. This is Jan. Jan Callahan."

"Jan, hi!" Susan smiled with pleasure.

"Is this a bad time?"

"No, not at all. Tom went into Austin today for a meeting with the education-finance committee, so it's pretty quiet here. Which is nice for a change," she added. "Gives me a chance to get caught up."

"Well, good. Listen, I won't keep you. I just wondered if you were free on Saturday."

"Saturday? You mean during the day?"

"No, Saturday night."

"Oh." Susan frowned in confusion. "Um, yes, I'm free then."

"Great. Patrick and I are going to have a little dinner party, and we'd like you to come."

"Oh." Now Susan was really taken aback. It had been a long time since she'd been invited to anything resembling a dinner party. In fact, except for invitations from Laverne, she hadn't been invited out socially since Paul's death. "Well, I, um...that's really nice of you. I'd love to come."

"Good. I'm also asking Patrick's brother, Keith, and Sophie and Tucker Temple and Jackie MacMillan and Alan Maravek. I know you know Keith, but how about the others?"

"I've met Sophie and Tucker. Their son plays soccer and he and Scott were on the same team last year. I've never met Jackie MacMillan or Alan Maravek, though." So Keith would be there. Was Jan thinking of them as a couple? Did that mean everyone in his family saw them that way? In a way, it was flattering, but Susan knew it wasn't a good idea to encourage the thought. She bit her lip. She should never have said she'd come to the party.

You're in dangerous waters. Getting in deeper and deeper. Get out now while you still can.

"Well, they're really nice," Jan said. "Jackie has a dancing school—my girls have all studied with her—and Alan is a tennis buddy of Patrick's. He works for a computer company in Austin."

While Jan was talking, Susan cast around for some reason to say she had been mistaken about being free and wouldn't be able to come to the dinner party after all. But she could think of nothing that wouldn't sound lame. Trouble was, she was a terrible liar. "Wh-what time were you thinking of?"

"Come around seven. On second thought, I'll ask Keith to pick you up. That way you won't have to come by yourself."

Susan opened her mouth to object, but before she could, Jan added breezily, "Well, I'd better not keep you. See you Saturday. I'm really looking forward to it." Then she broke the connection.

Susan stared at the phone for a long time before slowly replacing the receiver in the cradle. "How do I get myself in these predicaments?" she murmured.

You know how. When it comes to anything to do with Keith Callahan, you can't say no. The truth is, you want the impossible. And even though you know the impossible is impossible, you still think, deep in your heart, that somehow, some way, a miracle will happen. That's why you keep seeing Keith.

Susan buried her head in her hands. Suddenly she felt as if she were on an out-of-control train. It was hurtling through a tunnel, and at the end of the tunnel was a mountain. There was no way around the mountain. No miracle to save her. Nothing to prevent the monumental collision that awaited her at journey's end.

Chapter Eleven

Susan kept thinking about Saturday night. Keith coming to pick her up seemed too much like a date. *I'll call him and tell him it's not necessary.* She actually had her hand on the phone when she had second thoughts. Maybe that would be making too big a deal out of the whole thing. After all, they *were* friends. There was nothing wrong with two friends riding to a party together. Was there?

Torn by indecision, she did nothing. On Wednesday night he called her.

"I'll come by to get you about twenty minutes to seven on Saturday, okay?"

"All right." What else could she say?

"I'm looking forward to it," he added, his voice deepening.

Something warm slid through her. "Me, too." *God help me.*

For the next two days, Susan thought about nothing else. It had been such a long time since she'd gone out for the evening. Oh, she and Amy had gone to the movies a couple of times, but that was different.

Even Scott was excited. Because he thought he was too old for a babysitter, Susan made arrangements for him to spend Saturday night with his friend David. David's mother suggested Scott come early so they could go out for hamburgers together, so by four o'clock on Saturday, Susan was free to concentrate on getting ready.

She tried on at least six outfits before settling on a short black sheath. With it she wore the single-strand pearl necklace and matching earrings Laverne had given her on her thirtieth birthday. She hoped she wasn't too dressed up, yet it *was* a dinner party.

Even though she took her time with her hair and makeup, she was still ready far too early. Too nervous to read or watch TV while she waited for Keith, she paced around downstairs. Good thing Scott wasn't there, she thought ruefully. He would have thought his mother was crazy, the way she was acting.

When the doorbell rang a few minutes before six-forty, her heart gave a leap. She took several deep breaths before opening the door.

Oh, my, she thought at the sight of Keith. He looked incredibly handsome in a black dress shirt, black slacks, black jacket, and a burgundy silk tie.

"I call it my Mafia look," he said, grinning. "Nice dress," he added. His tone and eyes said a lot more.

She ducked her head. "Thanks." She knew she was blushing and could have kicked herself. Why *couldn't* she be one of those cool women who took compliments and admiration in their stride?

The drive to Patrick and Jan's home on the west side of town only took ten minutes. They pulled up in front of the sprawling ranch-style house just as another car did, and when its occupants got out, Susan recognized the Temples. Sophie Temple was a lovely woman, and Susan was glad to see her again. They all greeted each other and walked to the front door together.

"Well, hi!" Jan said, opening the door. She looked cute in a red dress and sparkly red earrings. Patrick, grinning broadly, stood behind her.

Susan was relieved to see that she wasn't overdressed at all. Sophie wore a silky blue dress, and her husband wore a jacket, just like Keith.

A few minutes later, the other two guests arrived. Together, Susan saw, so they must be a couple. That meant Jan *had* invited her for Keith. *Oh, you knew that already. Don't pretend you didn't.*

Jan introduced the newcomers to Susan and Keith, who obviously didn't know them, either. Susan liked Alan Maravek right away. He had an open, boyish face and a nice smile. She wasn't so sure about Jackie MacMillan. The woman was very attractive, with a lean, sinewy dancer's body, thick, curly black hair and startling green eyes, but there was something cold about her. She was polite to Susan but obviously not interested in her, and she quickly turned her attention to Keith.

"I've met several of your brothers now," she said in a low, throaty voice. She gave Keith an admiring smile. "What is it with you Callahans? You're all so *handsome.*"

Oh, barf, Susan thought.

Keith shrugged. "I think my brothers are pretty ugly, personally."

Patrick, who was standing a few feet away, said, "I heard that."

Keith laughed. "I said it for your benefit."

"Take it from me," Jackie said, linking her arm through Keith's, "you're wrong."

Even though Susan wanted to smack the woman, she turned to Jan and said brightly, "Jan, the house looks lovely. I love the paper here in the foyer, and that table is gorgeous. Where'd you get it?"

Jan answered as they all moved into the living room, where Patrick fixed drinks for everyone and Jan served appetizers. It quickly became apparent that something was wrong between Jackie and Alan, for she continued to ignore him. Susan felt sorry for him and when he walked over to talk to her—Keith was talking to Tucker Temple—she made an effort to be as warm and friendly as she could, even though normally she disliked making small talk with people she didn't know, especially men. He seemed pathetically grateful for her attention, almost too grateful, she thought uncomfortably, because he stuck close, even when she tried to move away to join Jan and

Sophie Temple, who were standing to one side talking animatedly.

In the meantime, Susan realized that Jackie had once again attached herself to Keith. Her entire body, clad in a body-skimming green sheath, had assumed a flirtatious stance and several times she laughed— the sound husky and provocative.

Susan wasn't sure how Keith was reacting to the attention, because after that first glance, she tried not to look in their direction. She certainly didn't want Keith to think she cared who he talked to. But every time she heard Jackie laugh, something inside her tightened.

Finally Jan said it was time to eat, and Keith broke away from Jackie and came to claim Susan. They walked into the dining room and Jan indicated where each should sit. Susan found herself seated between Keith and Alan with Jackie placed directly across the table from Keith.

Great, she thought. Just great.

The next two hours were agony for Susan. Jackie barely spoke to her or Jan, who sat on her right at the head of the table, and she paid no attention at all to Tucker on her other side. Instead, she concentrated her attention on Keith, addressing most of her remarks to him and laughing gaily at just about everything he said. By the time dessert was served, Susan wanted to strangle the woman. She was also less than enchanted with Keith, who certainly hadn't done anything to discourage Jackie. On some level she realized she was being unfair to him. After all, short of being downright rude to the woman, he could hardly do otherwise than answer her questions. And he *had* tried to include Susan in the conversation. Jackie was the one who excluded her.

Finally dinner was over. When Jan got up to begin clearing the table, Susan quickly stood, too. "I'll help you."

"Oh, no, Susan, that's not necessary. Patrick will help me."

"I insist," Susan said firmly, picking up her plate and Keith's. There was no way she was going to sit there one more minute.

When she and Jan reached the kitchen, Jan said, "Susan, I'm so sorry about Jackie. I don't know what's gotten into her tonight. I've never seen her act this way."

Susan shrugged. "It's no big deal. Please don't worry about it."

"Well, I think it's a big deal. She's been awful tonight, practically slobbering over Keith and completely ignoring everyone else. I know it's been uncomfortable for you."

"No, really, I'm fine. After all, it's not like Keith and I are a *couple* or anything. We're just friends, so if she's interested in him, he's perfectly free to pursue it. I don't care."

Jan put down the dishes she was carrying and stared at Susan. "You don't really mean that, do you?"

"Of course I do." Susan was proud of herself. She sounded very convincing and even managed to look Jan straight in the eye.

"I know Keith doesn't feel that way."

In spite of herself, Susan couldn't help saying, "You do? Why? Has...has he said something?"

Jan grinned. "No, but he was making eyes at you the entire evening at the spaghetti supper."

"Oh, he was not."

"He certainly was. Even Patrick thought so."

"You've discussed this with *Patrick?*"

"Don't worry. He won't say anything to Keith."

"I hope not, because I meant what I said, Jan. Keith are I are just friends. And that's the way it's going to remain."

Jan frowned. "Why? Don't you *like* him?"

"Yes, of course, I do, but..." She couldn't tell Jan the truth, and she couldn't think of a convincing lie, let alone carry it off. "Look, I really don't want to talk about this. Paul has only been gone nine months."

Jan looked stricken. "Oh, Susan, I'm sorry. I didn't mean to be insensitive. I just thought..."

"It's okay. I know you meant well." Susan smiled at her to show she wasn't angry or upset. "I'm not offended."

"I hope not. I—"

"Really. It's okay." Susan gave Jan a warm smile and after a moment the concern in Jan's eyes faded and she smiled back.

After that, they finished the clean-up, and when it was over Susan told Keith she had a headache and wanted to go home. He readily agreed, even seemed relieved to be leaving. Susan wondered if he would mention anything about Jackie, then decided he probably wouldn't. And she certainly didn't intend to. So on the ride home, she continued the fiction of the headache, and Keith considerately didn't try to make conversation. When they reached her house, she thanked him politely for giving her a ride and apologized for making him leave the party early.

"I don't mind at all. I'm just sorry you're not feeling well."

"I'll be fine once I take some Advil and get a good night's sleep."

He insisted on walking her to the door and waiting until she'd gotten it unlocked. Once she had, he hesitated for a moment, then bent down and brushed her cheek with his lips. "Sleep well," he murmured.

Inside, Susan leaned against the door, closing her eyes and listening to the sound of his car as he backed out of the driveway and drove off down the street.

It had been a mistake to go tonight. A mistake she'd be wise not to repeat.

"Jackie ruined everything!"

"No, she didn't," Patrick said patiently.

Jan put the last of the dishes into the dishwasher. "Yes, she did. She monopolized Keith, and I know Susan was upset, even though she said she wasn't. Why else do you think she wanted to leave early?"

"Because she had a headache."

"Headache! She didn't have a headache. She was tired of watching Jackie hanging all over Keith."

Patrick didn't answer for a moment. Finally he said, "Well, Jan, I warned you not to meddle, didn't I? Now I hope you've learned your lesson."

* * *

Autumn in Rainbow's End was Keith's favorite time of year. The heat of summer declined during September, yet the rainy, cold winter was still months away. And although the trees didn't have the variety of colors found in New England, there were enough maples, aspens, and red and Spanish oaks to turn the valley into a veritable feast for the eyes.

Throughout September and October, Keith spent as much time as possible with Scott and Susan. At least a couple of times a week, he would stop by on his way home from work. He never stayed too long; he didn't want Susan to feel obligated to invite him to eat with them. He'd be there just long enough to shoot a few baskets with Scott or, on the occasional rainy day, to play a game of checkers or to admire the antique cars.

While he was there, he would ask Susan if there was anything that needed doing around the house. At first, she always said no. But gradually, as she became more comfortable around him—and as the memory of the disastrous evening at Patrick's faded—she started allowing him to do some minor repairs, like oiling the squeaky screen door, or fixing a dripping faucet.

At least once a week, he invited them to go out for pizza or a hamburger. It was always a casual invitation. Keith constantly reminded himself that he had to take the relationship slow. Paul hadn't been dead a year yet.

But that wasn't the only reason. Susan was skittish. Whether her skittishness stemmed from their rocky past or from some other reason didn't matter.

If Keith pushed too hard, he could lose all chance of any kind of future with her, and he wasn't willing to risk that.

His feelings for Susan and Scott went too deep. They were too important to him to take any chance of losing them before he'd ever won them. So no matter how long it took, he would be patient. Right now his main goal was building Susan's trust as well as their friendship. For now, that was enough.

By October, Keith felt his campaign was gaining ground. Susan seemed glad to see him when he stopped by, and she always said yes to his invitations. He began to think about asking her out on a real date. Scott was going with his grandmother to California for a week. It would be the perfect time to try to see Susan alone.

He got his opportunity the following Wednesday. A friend of Scott's was at the house when Keith dropped by, so he had a few minutes alone with Susan.

"So Scott's leaving for California on Saturday?" he said.

She smiled. "Yes. He's so excited."

"I'll bet. You'll miss him, though."

"Yes, I will. But I guess I'd better start getting used to it. One of these days he'll be going off to college."

Keith laughed. "C'mon. He's only nine. He's got a ways to go before college."

Susan laughed sheepishly. "I know, but the time goes so fast. It's just unbelievable. Wait till you have kids. Then you'll see."

For some reason, she seemed flustered after saying this and wouldn't meet his eyes.

"Listen," he said, "I was thinking. How about if I take you out to dinner Saturday night? You know, somewhere only adults go. Maybe that new Italian place that opened up on the highway."

She looked up. "Saturday?"

"Yeah. Unless you have something else planned."

"No, I don't, but..." She seemed undecided about something. "Well, actually, there *is* something else...."

Keith felt a quick stab of jealousy. If she was going out with another guy...

"Saturday's the annual faculty dinner dance at the college," she said slowly. "I told my boss I wasn't going to go, but if you'd like to go with me..." Her voice trailed off uncertainly.

Keith grinned. "Sure, I'd like to go."

He whistled all the way home.

What is wrong with you?

Susan stared out the kitchen window. A squirrel darted up the trunk of the big oak tree on the other side of the driveway. It was quickly followed by another. Normally she enjoyed watched their antics. Today she hardly saw them.

Why had she asked Keith to the dinner dance? Hadn't she decided, after Jan's dinner party at the end of August, that she wouldn't make the same mistake again? That she would not go anywhere with Keith unless Scott was along? That she would not do anything that could even remotely be construed as a date?

You're going to be sorry.

Because this is a very bad idea.

Susan drove Laverne and Scott to the airport in Austin Saturday morning. Their ten o'clock flight left on time, and even though Susan spent several pleasant hours shopping in the city before heading for home, she was still back at the house by three, leaving her lots of time to get ready before Keith called for her at seven.

Her stomach tingled in anticipation, especially when she looked at the new dress she'd purchased that afternoon. It was the prettiest dress she'd ever owned—a shimmering column of gold with a long slit up the back. She'd really splurged on it. It cost far more than she should have spent, but the minute she'd seen it, she'd been unable to resist at least trying it on.

"Oh," the salesclerk said in admiration. "It looks wonderful on you."

And it did, Susan had thought as she twisted and turned to see herself in the three-way mirror. The gold silk brought out the gold highlights in her hair and the tawny flecks in her eyes.

And it was a perfect fit, just skimming her body, not too tight, not too loose. In it, Susan felt beautiful. More, she felt…sexy.

"I'll take it," she said, ignoring the little leap of guilt over the price.

She'd quickly gotten over the guilt. After all, she

was working and earning money. And she so seldom spent any on herself.

She took her time getting ready, indulging herself in a leisurely bubble bath, which was so deliciously soothing, it almost felt sinful. She washed and conditioned her hair, then set it on big rollers so that it would be easier to style. She used a scented body lotion that matched her favorite perfume.

She took great pains with her makeup, using a sparkly gold eye shadow and mascara and eyeliner. Foregoing her usual pink-toned lipstick, she put on a vivid red. When she finished her makeup, she worked on her hair, brushing it till it shone. She spritzed herself with perfume, put her diamond studs—a gift from Laverne the previous Christmas—in her ears, and finally, stepped into her dress.

It was a struggle to get the back zipped up by herself, but she managed. Then, heart beating a little too fast, she studied herself in the full-length mirror on her closet door. She hardly recognized the glamorous creature staring back. And although she was nervous and even a little scared, she was also excited—an excitement that hollowed out her stomach and made her feel the way she did when she looked down from a great height.

What would Keith think when he saw her? she wondered. She remembered how admiring he'd been the night they'd gone to dinner at Patrick and Jan's. She also remembered how that evening had ended. It was odd how they'd never talked about that episode. She certainly would never have brought it up, because she had no intention of ever letting Keith know how it had bothered her to have another woman flirt with him like that. And he obviously was pretending it had never happened.

Giving herself one final look in the mirror, she picked up her satin evening bag, turned out the bedroom lights and slowly walked downstairs to wait for Keith's arrival.

Keith was momentarily speechless at the sight of the breathtaking woman standing before him. He whistled softly. "Wow."

Susan smiled slowly. "Thanks. You look pretty nice yourself."

Keith self-consciously straightened his bow tie. "It's been a long time since I've worn a tux."

"I know. I haven't worn a long dress since high school. It's kind of fun to get dressed up, though, isn't it?"

He smiled. "Even though I'll probably get thrown out of the he-men club, I have to admit it *is* fun. Well. You ready to go?"

"Yes." Susan walked over to retrieve her purse and a black velvet jacket, which were lying on a small antique table in the entryway.

Watching her, Keith sucked in his breath. What was it about a slit skirt that was so sexy? He'd seen more of Susan's legs when she wore shorts, yet the flash of leg exposed by the slit in her skirt was a real turn-on. Hell, be honest, he thought, everything about Susan was a real turn-on.

Keith reached for the jacket and helped her put it on, then held her arm lightly as they walked outside.

Her skin felt firm and warm, and the gossamer fragrance of her perfume drifted around him seductively, making his head spin.

How did she do it? he wondered. She wasn't a flirt. She wasn't what you'd call a babe. She was just a pretty, girl-next-door type, wholesome and nice. And yet she turned him on as no other woman ever had.

But his feelings weren't just about sex, although he certainly wanted her. No, what he felt for her went way beyond sex. He liked her and he liked being with her. She made him feel good.

In addition—and maybe most significantly—she aroused all kinds of protective feelings in him. He wanted to take care of her and Scott—wanted to make sure nothing ever hurt them again. He had never felt that way about any other woman.

Ruefully, he remembered how he had teased Paul about "having it bad." The tables had certainly turned, because Keith now had it bad himself.

He wished he knew how Susan felt about him. He was sure she liked being with him. But did her feelings go deeper? He wished he could just come right out and ask her, but he knew it was still too soon.

Be patient. Things have been going well lately. Don't push your luck.

"Did you buy a new car?" Susan said as he opened the passenger door of Rory's BMW and helped her in.

"No. I borrowed this from Rory."

"Just for tonight?"

"Yep." He closed her door and walked around to

the driver's side. Once they were on their way, he said, "I couldn't see us going to a fancy dinner dance in my sorry old truck."

"I wouldn't have minded."

He glanced at her briefly before turning his eyes back to the road. She wouldn't have minded, either, he knew. Susan didn't care about superficial things. That was one of the things he liked most about her. "Well, I minded."

"This *is* a nice car."

He smiled. "Yep, nothing but the best for Rory."

They were silent for a few minutes, then Keith said, "Did Scott get off all right?"

Susan laughed. "Yes, you should have seen him. He was so excited he was up an hour before the alarm went off. He couldn't wait."

Keith chuckled. "I used to be the same way when I was going somewhere."

"I still am."

For a while they talked about Scott and the trip. When the conversation died off, Keith put on a Bonnie Raitt CD and they listened to the music until they reached the Rainbow's End Inn where the dinner dance was being held. You couldn't miss the place. It was lit up like a Christmas tree, with hundreds of tiny white lights twinkling from the branches of the trees surrounding the stone structure.

"It's so pretty, don't you think?" Susan said. "I love the lights. They keep them up all year round."

"Yeah, that's a nice touch."

Keith pulled into the circular driveway in front.

"We're sitting with my boss tonight," Susan said. "Do you mind?"

"No. I'm looking forward to meeting him."

"Good. I think you'll like him."

Keith surrendered the keys to the valet-parking attendant and, filled with pride, possessively held Susan's waist as they walked into the inn. It was with reluctance that he released her when they walked inside. They were immediately greeted by a pretty, dark-haired hostess who showed them to the private room where the party was being held.

Keith had never been to the inn before. It had been built after he'd moved to Alaska, but he was impressed. The room they entered was large enough to hold a couple of hundred people comfortably, although there weren't that many there so far tonight. He looked around. At one end of the room was a massive stone fireplace; at the other there was a slightly raised bandstand. Across the room, on the other side from the arched entrance, open terrace doors looked out over a beautiful back garden filled with paths that wound through the trees and flower beds. "This is a really nice place."

"It is, isn't it? You know, when it was being built, I wondered if our area could support a facility like this, but they're busy all the time. They do a great restaurant business, and this room is constantly booked—for weddings and all kinds of parties."

"I can see why." Keith made a mental note to ask his father who had done the construction on the place, for the workmanship was excellent.

Susan looked around. "There's Tom." Reaching

for Keith's hand, she led him off to a large table in the center of the room.

Keith liked Tom Shaver immediately. There was something about the big man that made it impossible not to like him. And Shaver's wife, Monica, was just as nice, with a sweet smile and friendly green eyes.

"Well, Susan," Shaver said with a chuckle, "you sure clean up good."

"Tom!" his wife said in a horrified tone.

"Ah, she knows what I mean," Shaver said.

"You look lovely, my dear," Monica Shaver said, rolling her eyes at her husband.

"Thank you," Susan said, laughing. "So do you. That's a beautiful dress."

"Thank you." Monica smoothed the skirt of her red chiffon gown with a pleased smile.

"It should be beautiful. It cost enough," her husband said.

They all laughed. For the next few minutes, they talked easily. Soon they were joined by another couple—a plumpish brunette with a lively smile and a tall, sandy-haired man. Susan introduced them as Rhonda Berringer and her husband Dave. "Rhonda's our office manager," Susan explained.

"And chief whip cracker," added Shaver, eyes twinkling affectionately.

"Some whip cracker," Rhonda said. "I can't even get you to work on time." She turned to Keith. "It's nice to meet you, Keith." Her eyes were filled with curiosity as they gave him a quick assessment.

He grinned and almost asked her if he'd passed inspection.

After handshakes and greetings all round, the six of them settled at the table, which was set for eight.

"Who else will be joining us?" Susan asked.

"Jamie and her date," Rhonda said.

"Jamie's our clerk," Susan told Keith. "She's really cute. You'll like her." She glanced up and smiled. "Here she comes now."

Keith was introduced to a pretty redhead who was accompanied by a tall boy who looked no older than eighteen, but was probably in his twenties. He smiled shyly.

The room was filling with people and getting noisier by the minute. Many of them stopped by their table and they all seemed to know Susan and like her. Once again pride filled Keith as he watched her. The self-consciousness she sometimes displayed in his company was not in evidence tonight. Instead, she was clearly in her element. Suddenly, he was filled with resolve.

Whatever it took, he wanted this woman for his own—not just tonight, but every night.

Chapter Twelve

Drink orders were taken, and soon after, dinner service began with small Caesar salads, followed by bowls of mushroom soup, then the main course, which consisted of stuffed chicken breasts, au gratin potatoes, and green beans.

The food was very good. Keith could see why the place was popular. Plus, it was served in generous amounts, which made Keith happy, for he was hungry. The company was working on a new apartment project, and Keith's dad wanted to finish while they still had good weather, so Keith and his brothers had been putting in long hours. It seemed like a long time since he'd had lunch.

Everyone at their table ate enthusiastically, even the women. Keith liked that. He hated when women picked at their food. He was glad Susan wasn't like that. She had a healthy appetite and still managed to keep slim.

He knew she worked out. Several times she'd mentioned riding her stationary bike or walking on the treadmill. He liked that about her, too, that she took care of herself.

In addition to the good meal, conversation was lively throughout dinner. Shaver and his wife and Rhonda and her husband were all talkers who kept the ball going without any awkward gaps. By the time dessert—an excellent chocolate mousse—was served, Keith was thoroughly enjoying himself. These were nice people, he decided, people he would enjoy getting to know better. He was glad for Susan, since she was the one who had to work with them every day.

Once the dessert plates were cleared, the band, a quartet of musicians on keyboard, guitar, drums and bass, began to play. Midway through the first number, a bouncy swing tune, Keith realized they were pretty good and said so.

"Yes," Shaver agreed, "they're making a name for themselves in Austin music circles. We were lucky to get them." He smiled at Jamie. "And the credit for that goes to Jamie."

"The drummer's my brother," she explained with a proud smile.

"Well, they're great," Keith said, tapping his foot.

After two more fast numbers, the band segued into a slow tune, something softly romantic, and Keith asked Susan if she'd like to dance.

She smiled. "I'd love to."

They moved out onto the dance floor, and he drew her into his arms. Keith liked to dance, and he was pretty good, the result of a lot of effort on the part of his mother, who believed all boys needed to know how to dance. Susan was a natural, he decided. She followed him with ease, and they glided around the dance floor seamlessly, the way couples do who have danced together for years.

"You're a good dancer," she said.

"Thanks. That was one of the things my mother insisted we learn to do."

Showing off a little, he twirled her around. Her eyes sparkled with pleasure and something else, something Keith was feeling, too. He tightened his hold, bringing her closer. Holding her like this, Keith found it harder and harder to breathe. Whoever had invented dancing was a sadist, he decided, because the sensations pummeling him were sheer torture. All he could think about was how much he wanted Susan. And from the way she was responding to him, he was sure she felt the same way.

Maybe tonight...

He was afraid to finish the thought, afraid he'd jinx himself. But he couldn't help hoping, because it was getting harder and harder to be patient.

Susan knew the way she felt was dangerous, but she couldn't seem to control her reactions tonight. Her defenses were becoming weaker with every passing moment. But for some reason, right now she simply didn't care. She nestled her head under

Keith's chin, closed her eyes, and gave herself up to the sensations.

If only they could stay this way forever, she thought dreamily. Safe in the cocoon of the dance floor, where it was acceptable to hold each other. If only they never had to emerge into the real world where harsh realities would always keep them apart.

Don't think about reality. Just enjoy the moment.

But the moment couldn't last. Moments never did. They ended, and new moments took their place. So it was with this moment. The set ended, and the band once more struck up a fast song, which Susan didn't feel comfortable with, so they headed back to their table.

For the rest of the evening Susan was acutely aware of Keith beside her. Even when they were both talking to someone else, she felt his nearness.

Dancing with him was excruciating: half pleasure, half pain. Toward the end of the evening, as they were once more dancing to a slow, romantic song, she knew with certainty that she'd been right. It had been a big mistake to invite him tonight. Being held in his arms like this, feeling what she was feeling, was only going to make the future harder for her, because with every passing second, she realized more and more what she was missing. What she would always be missing.

The sensible part of her wanted the evening over, so she could go home and end this agony. But the other part of her, the foolish, romantic, cries-at-sad-movies, happily-ever-after-in-spite-of-all-odds part of her, wanted it to go on forever.

"Let's go outside," Keith murmured as the number ended.

Say no. It's just asking for trouble to go out there with him. "All right."

Together, they walked out the terrace doors and down the steps onto the garden path. The evening air was cool, raising goose bumps on Susan's arms.

"You're cold," Keith said.

"A little."

"Here." He took off his jacket.

"But now *you'll* be cold," she protested.

"Not me. I'm fine." He draped the jacket over her shoulders, and somehow his arm just seemed to settle there naturally when he was finished.

Susan's heart beat faster. Oh, she was definitely in trouble. And yet it was so wonderful to walk in this beautiful place, close together, just the two of them, away from everyone else. It was really a perfect ending to a perfect evening. As they walked farther along the winding path, the sound of the band faded into the background, and she became more aware of the night noises surrounding them: a mockingbird singing in a tree, crickets chirping nearby, cicadas buzzing. The moon was a silvery arc high above. All so lovely...so romantic...

When they reached the farthest point in the garden, they were on the other side of the inn and could no longer see their fellow party-goers or be seen by them. Keith's arm tightened around her.

"Susan," he said softly, turning her to face him.

Heart drumming, she looked up. His eyes gleamed in the moonlight. She swallowed. He was going to kiss her. She could see the intention in his eyes. And even though she knew it was utter and complete madness, she also knew she was going to let him.

His head dipped.

She closed her eyes.

Their lips met and clung. Her senses reeled as the kiss deepened, and he pulled her closer still. All conscious thought stopped. There was only Keith and the reawakened desire to be his. The primitive need to take and be taken.

And yet, even as his hands skimmed over her body, even as she strained to meet them, even as her heart was saying *yes,* her head knew they had to stop before things went too far.

From somewhere she found the strength to push away, to say, in a voice that didn't sound like hers, ''We'd better go back inside.''

She thought he would protest and she tried to think what she would say. But he didn't, and she was very grateful, for her defenses were too fragile to have withstood any kind of argument. Yet there was a small part of her that wondered why he'd given in so easily. Didn't he *want* to make love to her?

He didn't try to talk to her as they walked back to the party, and Susan used the few minutes to attempt to get herself under control.

When they reached the terrace doors, she shrugged out of his jacket and handed it to him. ''Do you mind if we leave now?'' She tried, but couldn't meet his eyes.

''That's fine with me.''

Susan's emotions were chaotic all the while they

were driving home. Why had she gone outside with him tonight? Kissed him like that? What must he think of her? What must he think, period? He probably thought she was a tease, kissing him like that, then suddenly stopping. Her face felt hot. She snuck glances at him out of the corner of her eye. His face revealed nothing, but he must be thinking about what had happened.

Susan, you're a fool.

She bit her lip. Closed her eyes. Thought about that kiss. Thought about how much she wanted him. He wanted her, too. She knew he did.

Scott's away.

The thought had been at the back of her mind all night. And it would be so easy, when they got to the house, just to take Keith's hand and lead him inside and up the stairs to her bedroom.

She shivered. The force of her desire nearly overwhelmed her. Yet to yield to it would be absolute madness. Their situation was complicated enough, and making love with Keith again would only complicate it further, because nothing could ever come of it.

You always knew you were playing with fire.

She felt like crying.

No matter how much she wanted to, she couldn't allow it to happen. She'd made one mistake already tonight. She couldn't make another one.

Keith pulled the car into Susan's driveway and cut the ignition. On the silent drive home, he had made up his mind. It was obvious Susan was upset. He wasn't sure why, because it was also obvious she'd wanted to kiss him. So her reaction had to have something to do with their past. Did she think he would run out on her again? Was that it? Or was she feeling disloyal to Paul?

He realized they needed to talk, *really* talk, not just brush over what had happened ten years ago the way they had that night at the pizza place. And tonight, with Scott away, was the perfect opportunity.

Wordlessly, they walked to the front door. When they reached it, she opened her purse and took out her key. "Thank you for taking me tonight, Keith. It was a lovely evening."

So she wasn't going to ask him in. Well, he wasn't going to let her run away. "Are we going to pretend what happened between us tonight didn't happen?" he said softly.

For a long moment she said nothing. Then she sighed and looked up. "It might be best if we did."

"Mind telling me why you feel that way?"

"Because it shouldn't have happened."

"Why not? You wanted me to kiss you just as much as I did, didn't you?"

"Yes, I—I admit I did, but..." She paused. "Look, Keith, despite what happened between us all those years ago, I am not the kind of woman who can have a casual sexual relationship."

"I never thought you were. That's not what I want, either. Look, Susan...I hadn't planned to say this tonight, because I didn't want to rush you. But I can't have you thinking that all I want from you is sex." He took a deep breath. "I love you. I've always loved you. I want to marry you."

She stared at him. She looked stricken.

God, he was such an idiot! He shouldn't have just blurted that out. Laying his hands on her shoulders, he spoke urgently. "I know you probably don't trust me yet, and I don't blame you. After running out on you the way I did... I've always been sorry about that. You know, back then, I was young and immature and scared, and I thought going away was the only thing I could do. I know now that running off like that was cowardly. I should have stayed, been honest with Paul and taken my chances. Who knows? Maybe you still would have chosen Paul instead of me, but at least I would have tried."

She bowed her head, not saying anything for a long moment. Finally she looked up. "Thank you for telling me that, Keith. I appreciate it, but it doesn't change things. I-I'm sorry, but I don't think we should see each other anymore."

"You can't mean that."

"I—I'm afraid I do."

"But why?"

"Because it...it's hopeless. It can never work out between us."

"Of course it can."

"No. No, it can't."

"I don't understand why not. Are you still angry with me about the past?"

"No, that's not it at all."

"Well, what then?"

"It won't work because I—I don't love you."

He stared at her. She didn't mean that. She couldn't.

"I—I'm sorry. I didn't mean to lead you on."

"I don't believe you. I know you, Susan. You couldn't have kissed me the way you did if you didn't have feelings for me."

"If you choose not to believe me, that's your prerogative. The kiss tonight was just the result of too much champagne and…and no sex for months. I—I've always been sexually attracted to you—after all, look what happened to us all those years ago—but sex isn't love. And it's certainly no basis for marriage."

Her words were like knives, cutting deeply. "I can't believe you're saying this. I can't believe you mean it."

"I'm sorry. I—I do mean it."

Suddenly he was furious. What the hell kind of game had she been playing with him? "What's *really* going on here? Am I not *good* enough for you? Are you afraid you'll lose out on the Sheridan money if you marry me? Is that it?"

She stared at him. For a moment, he thought she was going to say something in her defense. When she didn't, he finally realized what a fool he'd been, because her silence spoke volumes.

"Never mind," he said coldly. "I have my answer."

Giving her one last contemptuous look, he spun on his heel and walked away.

He didn't look back.

* * *

Susan managed to hold herself together until she reached her bedroom. Then, sick at heart, she threw herself across her bed and let the tears come.

Why, why? she asked herself over and over again. Why must life be so unfair? She thought about how Keith had said he realized he shouldn't have run away ten years ago. How he wished he'd stayed, been honest with Paul, and taken his chances. Oh, if only he had! If only he had. Things would have turned out so differently.

But he hadn't. And now it was too late for them. The clock could never be turned back. They could never be together.

She had been playing with fire in the past months, and tonight, she'd come dangerously close to leaping into the middle of the flames—into a place where there would be no rescue. So even though it had been agony pretending she didn't care for Keith, she had done what she had to do, and now Keith hated her.

She couldn't even have him as a friend.

How was she going to bear it?

The first thing Keith did when he walked into his town house was open the cupboard where he kept his supply of liquor. He poured himself a tumbler of J&B, then proceeded to drink himself into a stupor.

He still couldn't believe what had happened. How could he have been so wrong about Susan? Man, whoever it was that had said you can't go home again sure knew what he was talking about. He sure as hell should never have come back. That had been mistake number one.

Mistake number two had been apologizing to Susan, but what *really* galled him was the way he'd bared his soul to her, told her he loved her and asked her to marry him, and how she'd thrown the offer back in his face.

Sex isn't love, and it certainly is no basis for marriage.

Damn her! Damn all women. You couldn't trust any of them. They gave you these soft looks and they made you think they cared about you and then—wham!—they really stuck it to you.

Downing his drink, he poured another. He'd thought Susan was different. He'd have bet money that she was completely honest and straight.

He smiled cynically. Just went to show that even a normally savvy guy like him could be taken for a ride. Well, he'd learned his lesson. From now on, he was swearing off all women.

His thoughts tumbled on in this vein for the better part of two hours before the scotch finally put him to sleep. His last conscious thought was that there was no longer any reason for him to stay in Rainbow's End.

Susan awakened with a raging headache and swollen eyes. She took one look at herself in the mirror and decided she would skip church services. That's all she'd need, for someone to tell her mother-in-law that she was seen looking like this.

I'll stay home and clean the oven and refrigerator instead.

These were both jobs she hated and had been putting off for months. But today they seemed a fitting penance and exactly what she deserved.

Keith didn't wake up until noon. He was stiff and sore from sleeping on the couch, and his head was pounding like someone had put a sledgehammer to it. And he was still in the tux.

God, he thought in disgust. He was a mess. Slowly, he sat up, then cautiously made his way into the kitchen, where he found the bottle of Advil. He downed three, because this was a granddaddy of hangovers and needed serious help. Then he headed for his bedroom.

An hour later, showered and shaved and dressed in clean jeans and a sweatshirt, he padded out to the kitchen and put on a pot of coffee. Standing at the counter waiting for it to finish dripping, he thought about last night's decision to leave Rainbow's End and go back to Alaska.

Sure, that would eliminate him ever having to see Susan again, but what about Scott? Scott considered Keith to be his friend, and Keith really cared about the kid. Was it right to abandon Scott just because Susan had turned out to be someone other than the person Keith had thought she was? After all, Scott was an innocent bystander in all this. He didn't deserve to be hurt, and he would be hurt if Keith left. And the kid had been hurt enough in the past year.

Besides, Keith didn't really want to leave Rainbow's End again. Rainbow's End was his home. Being back like this, he'd realized that he'd missed it all these years.

Anger began to mount again.

He'd be *damned* if he'd let Susan drive him away.

"I'm not goin' anywhere," he said aloud. "Let *her* leave town if she's uncomfortable around me, because I'm not going to stop seeing Scott, either. So she'll just have to deal with it!"

It was the middle of the afternoon when Susan remembered Scott.

"Oh, no," she said, clapping her hand over her mouth. What was Scott going to say when Keith no longer came around? He adored Keith! He would be devastated.

Fresh tears pooled in her eyes. She put down the scouring pad she'd been using on the bottom of the oven and sat down at the kitchen table.

You should have thought about Scott a lot earlier. Like before you asked Keith to the dinner dance.

She sat there a long time, just staring into space and wishing she could turn the clock back.

What was she going to tell Scott?

By Wednesday Keith's anger had faded. It was replaced by a mixture of frustration and confusion. Something just didn't add up. He couldn't have been that wrong about Susan. She didn't care about the Sheridan money. He'd stake his life on that.

And she *was* honest.

Yet he knew she hadn't told him the truth when she'd said that all she felt for him was sexual attraction. She liked him. She liked being with him. Over the past months, they'd forged a real friendship.

But obviously, there was *some* reason she felt she couldn't marry him. He might have understood if Scott didn't like him and Susan was worried about how Scott would react if she and Keith married, but Scott sure wasn't a problem. Keith and Scott got along like a house afire. Why, Keith couldn't care more about Scott if he'd been his *own* kid, and Susan knew it.

So what the hell *was* it?

Since he could come up with no answers and knew he would have no opportunity to see Susan again until Scott came home, he tried not to think about her for the rest of the week. He was only marginally successful. Days were easier than nights. He was busy during the day, and lucky, too, he supposed. The kind of work he did, and the people he did it with, weren't conducive to contemplation or deep thinking.

But at night...that was a different story. Every evening he wondered what she was doing. Every evening, he had to fight to keep from driving past her house. And late at night, when he was in bed trying to go to sleep, was the worst time of all. Because then the thoughts of her refused to be banished. And with the thoughts came the wanting and the frustration.

By Saturday he was strung tighter than a fiddle string. He found himself snapping at people for no good reason.

"Hey," Rory said, frowning after the second time Keith had said something sarcastic in answer to a question, "what kind of bug you got up *your* butt?"

Keith bit back a sharp reply. Sighing, he said, "Sorry. I don't know what my problem is."

Rory gave him a funny look, but he didn't pursue the subject.

A few minutes later, Patrick pulled him aside. "Rory tells me you might want to talk."

Keith looked at his brother. It would feel good to unburden himself. And Patrick, being married, was probably the best one of his brothers to give him advice. "Let's knock off for lunch, okay? There *is* something I'd like to ask you about."

They climbed into Patrick's car and drove to their favorite hamburger joint. Over burgers and Cokes, Keith told Patrick the whole story. He concluded with, "If I thought she was telling me the truth, I could accept it. At least, I think I could. But I don't believe her." He looked at Patrick hopefully. "Now I don't know what to do."

Patrick gave him a wry smile. "You know," he said slowly, "just because I'm married doesn't mean I understand women."

Keith couldn't help it. He laughed.

"You should talk to Jan," Patrick said. "After all, *she's* a woman. She probably knows exactly what's going on in Susan's mind."

Keith shook his head. "No, I don't think so. I think I'd better work this out myself."

"All right. It's up to you. I won't say anything to Jan, either, you don't have to worry about that."

Keith smiled. "Thanks, bro. I appreciate you listening."

Patrick shrugged. ''Sorry I couldn't be of more help.''

Throughout the afternoon, Keith's mood was vastly improved, even though nothing had changed. It had just felt good to unburden himself. He even accepted Glenn's invitation to drive into Austin that evening. While there, Keith saw an advertisement for the circus, which was coming to town the following week. Perfect, he thought. The perfect reason to call Susan's house tomorrow.

The next day, he waited until noon before calling. He got the answering machine and left a message.

Two hours later, an excited Scott called him back.

''Hey, Scott. Did you have a good time in California?''

''Yeah, it was great!'' The boy proceeded to tell him all about the trip.

When Scott was done, Keith told him about the circus. ''So what do you think? Want to go?''

''Yeah! But I need to ask my mom.''

The boy obviously did not trouble to cover the phone, because every word said between them carried clearly, and Keith heard Susan say it was all right for Scott to go to the circus next Saturday.

''Keith? I can go!''

Keith smiled at Scott's unbridled enthusiasm and his penchant for talking in exclamation points. ''Great. I'll call for tickets, then give you a call back and let you know about the time, okay?''

''Okay!''

Twenty minutes later, tickets purchased, Keith called Scott back. Keith hoped Susan would answer the phone, but she didn't. Afraid it was me, he thought wryly.

"How would it be if I pick you up about five?" he asked Scott. "We can drive into Austin, get some pizza or a hamburger or something, and then go to the circus."

"Okay!" Scott said. "This is gonna be so cool!"

After they hung up, Keith smiled. For the first time in a week, he felt optimistic.

Chapter Thirteen

Susan was on pins and needles all week. Knowing she would see Keith on Saturday, both when he picked Scott up and when he brought him home again, was enough to affect her concentration to the point where she had to constantly talk to herself.

Even Rhonda commented on Susan's state of mind, saying on Wednesday, "Susan, is something wrong?"

Susan's head jerked around. She'd been staring out the window, something she'd done far too much for the past couple of days. "No. Nothing's wrong. Why do you ask?"

Rhonda shrugged. "I don't know. You just seemed…preoccupied. Worried."

Susan sighed. "Sorry. Guess I was daydreaming."

"You don't have to apologize. I just thought if there was anything wrong, well, maybe I could help."

"Thank you, Rhonda. I appreciate the offer. But really, there's nothing the matter."

After Rhonda walked back to her office, Susan told herself to shape up. This would never do.

If the days were bad, the nights were impossible. Susan, who had never had a problem sleeping, suddenly found herself lying awake until well after midnight. She would turn her pillow over, try moving into a different position, try thinking of something pleasant like what she would do if she won a million dollars—anything to lull her into sleep.

Nothing worked.

Images of Keith kept superimposing themselves over everything else. She played and replayed the night of the dinner dance. Lived the kiss they'd shared over and over again. Remembered the feel of his hands against her skin. Remembered how it had felt to dance close to him. And each time she did, she ached with longing.

Keith, oh Keith…

Why had she invited him to the dance? Why had she put herself in a position where her defenses would be so lowered that she would succumb to the desire she had imagined she could continue to manage?

Now that the desire had been unleashed, her body cried out for Keith—for his touch, for his kisses, for the fire and wonder they'd once shared.

For years she hadn't allowed herself to think about

that night so long ago. Now it was all she thought about. Sex with Paul had been sweet, comforting, even satisfying. But there'd been no shooting stars, no fireworks, no burning passion that simply had to be quenched or you would die of it, the way there'd been with Keith.

She remembered once when she and Paul had been married for a couple of years. It was a Saturday night and they'd gone out for dinner—Scott was spending the night at Laverne's—and when they came home Susan knew Paul would want to make love. He always wanted to make love on Saturday nights. She never refused him, no matter how she felt. After all, she owed Paul a lot, more than she could ever repay.

Afterwards, she'd been lying in the circle of his arms and he'd kissed her forehead and told her how much he loved her and how glad he was that they were together. She had smiled and murmured something back, but she'd been filled with the most unbearable sadness, because even then, and despite his goodness to her, she knew she still didn't love him the way she should, not the way he loved her.

Not the way she would have loved Keith.

She acknowledged that fact now, even as she'd buried it then.

Finally Saturday came.

It turned out to be a beautiful day: crisp, cool and sunny. Susan spent the morning doing laundry and other chores indoors, then headed outside to work in the flower beds. Scott and a couple of his friends were playing in the tree house, and all the while she worked, she could hear their laughter. The sound comforted her, but it still didn't take her mind off the awareness that very soon she would see Keith again.

How would he act? she wondered.

He would be polite, she knew. He was too much of a gentleman to be otherwise. But what would be in his eyes? Contempt? Dislike? Or would they simply be cold?

Oh, Keith, I'm so sorry.

At three o'clock, she went inside to get cleaned up. After showering and changing clothes, she called Scott indoors so that he would be ready when Keith arrived. While he was bathing, she fixed her hair and put on her makeup. Then she wiped half of it off. It would be best to look as if she hadn't made any special effort on Keith's account. She didn't want to send him mixed signals. She certainly didn't want to behave as if his coming to the house was special to her.

By five o'clock, she was a nervous wreck. She was telling herself to calm down when the front doorbell rang.

"I'll get it!" Scott cried, racing to the door.

Susan took a deep breath and walked slowly toward the foyer. Her heart pounded, and her hands felt clammy. *He'll only be here for a few minutes. Just a few minutes. And if you don't say much, you'll be okay. Just act normal.*

Keith, in jeans and a royal-blue sweater the same shade as his eyes, looking more handsome than any man had a right to look, was standing in the foyer.

At the sound of her footsteps, he looked up, and their eyes met.

"Hi." He didn't smile, but his gaze was not unfriendly.

She could hardly breathe, but somehow she managed to get out a weak "Hi." Walking over to the closet, she removed Scott's jacket and handed it to him, avoiding additional eye contact with Keith. Her heart was beating so hard she was sure he could hear it.

Scott screwed up his face. "Aw, Mom, do I hafta wear that?"

"Yes, I think you'd better. It's supposed to get colder tonight."

"I've got *my* jacket in the car," Keith said.

"Oh, okay." Scott happily put the jacket on.

Keith's eyes met hers over Scott's head, and there was an amused twinkle in them. "I'm not sure what time we'll be back tonight," he said.

"It doesn't matter. I'll be here." Looking at him, looking at the two of them—the man and the boy— Susan was seized with the most desperate longing. She would have given anything to be going with them. For the three of them to be a family. The longing was so intense, she was suddenly afraid everything she was thinking and feeling would show in her eyes. To cover her confusion, she put her arm around Scott and kissed his forehead. "'Bye, honey. Have a good time."

"'Bye, Mom." But he was already pulling away, impatient to be gone.

"'Bye, Susan," Keith said. He put his hand on

Scott's shoulder and gave her a parting smile. Together he and Scott walked out the door.

She stood in the open doorway and watched them. The lump in her throat was as big as Texas. Father and son, she thought. The man I love and the son we created together. And neither of them can ever know.

Stop thinking about it, Susan. What's done is done. No amount of agonizing will undo it.

All right, she thought determinedly. She would put all thoughts of Keith and their impossible situation out of her mind for the rest of the evening. She would use the time Scott was away to do something productive, something she'd been meaning to do for months without finding the time.

Heading for the spare bedroom which doubled as a home office, she took out the new Rolodex she'd bought, her old address book, and set to work.

"So what do you think?" Keith said about halfway through the performance. "You like it?"

"Yeah, it's *great!*" Scott said, bouncing in his seat. "Boy, look at that!" He pointed to the center ring where three elephants had just stood up on their back legs, holding the pose for long moments. The crowd cheered as the trainer put them through their paces.

"Amazing, isn't it?" But Keith wasn't really looking at the elephants. It was more fun to watch Scott. Every emotion was clearly etched on his face. As he had so many times before, Keith thought about how great it would be to have Scott as a son.

And if I could just convince Susan to marry me, he could be my son.

She had been nervous tonight. Nervous and embarrassed. Hell, he'd been nervous himself, although he felt he'd done a pretty good job of not showing it. Until he'd actually seen her, he hadn't been sure how he'd act or what he'd say. Then, when he did see her, he had decided to just cool it. It wasn't the time or the place to say anything personal, anyway.

"Keith! Look!"

Scott's exclamation snapped Keith out of his thoughts, and he saw what had excited the boy: the high-wire performers were climbing up the ladder in preparation for their performance.

For the next twenty minutes, Keith gave his full attention to the high-wire act, which was terrific. When it was over, the house lights came up. It was intermission.

"Want some popcorn or something?"

"Yeah," Scott said with an enthusiastic smile.

They made their way to the concession area and after some thought, Scott decided he wanted popcorn and orange soda. Keith settled on peanuts and a Coke. Once they'd gotten and paid for their snacks, they started back toward their seats.

"Keith!"

Keith turned at the sound of his name. At first he didn't see who it was who had called to him. Then he smiled, recognizing the pretty blonde walking toward him. Lorrie Carmichael was a former high-school classmate. He hadn't seen her in years. Someone had told him she'd moved to Austin.

"Hey, Lorrie," he said.

"I thought that was you." She gave him a pleased smile. "It's great to see you."

"Yeah, you, too." He'd always liked Lorrie. She'd been a cheerleader and lots of fun.

"And this must be your son."

Keith started to say no, he was the son of a friend, but Lorrie kept talking.

"I would have known him anywhere," she said, smiling down at Scott. "He looks just like you, especially those eyes." She laughed. "My God, those Callahan eyes. They're like a trademark."

Keith gave an embarrassed laugh. "Uh, Lorrie, this is Scott Sheridan. He's Paul Sheridan's son, not mine. You remember Paul, don't you?"

"Oh!" She frowned. "Really?" She smiled uncertainly. "Gee, now I feel stupid."

"No, don't. I guess it was a natural mistake, you know, seeing us together."

She nodded. "I heard that Paul—"

"Yeah," Keith said, interrupting her. Without actually looking at Scott, he gave her a meaningful look.

She obviously got the message that he didn't want to talk about Paul in front of Scott, because she smiled brightly and said, "So what are you doing now? Bob Howard told me you were living in Alaska."

"I was, but I've moved back home now. I'm working for my dad."

"Married?"

"Nope. How about you?"

She nodded happily. "Seven years now. I have twin boys. They're six."

They talked awhile longer, then Lorrie said she had to get back to her family. Keith and Scott returned to their seats, and soon after, the lights dimmed, and the second half of the performance started.

Keith thought about Lorrie's comment. Funny, he mused, studying Scott, but she was right. Scott *did* look kind of like a Callahan. Yeah, he could see why she'd assumed he was. *I wish,* he thought.

I wish.

At eight-thirty Susan finished writing the last address on a card and inserted it into the Rolodex. Then, sighing, she stretched. Her back and neck muscles ached from sitting at the desk all evening. But at least the Rolodex was finished.

Gee, she thought wryly, I should be unhappy in my love life all the time. I'd sure get a lot of jobs done around the house.

Her stomach growled, and she remembered that she hadn't eaten any dinner. Getting up, she decided she would go downstairs and make herself a cup of tea and a turkey sandwich. She was halfway down the stairs when the phone rang. For a second, she debated whether to go back upstairs and answer it in her bedroom or continue on downstairs and answer it in the kitchen. She was closer to the bedroom, so that made her decision.

She caught the phone on the fourth ring. "Hello," she said, slightly breathless.

"Susan?"

"Yes?"

"Susan, this is Birdie Collier."

"Oh, hi, Birdie." Birdie Collier was one of Laverne's friends, part of a bridge foursome who had played together for years.

"Susan, I'm at the hospital. Laverne has had a heart attack."

"Oh, my God! Is she all right? Wh-when? How?" Shock caused her to stumble over her words.

"Listen. Calm down. They've got her stabilized, although she's in the critical-care unit. We were playing bridge tonight, you know, the way we always do, and we'd just had our dessert and started playing when she suddenly gripped her chest. It was pretty scary, because she turned gray in the space of seconds. But thank God, Marian—you know Marian Schuler, don't you? Well, Marian kept her head and immediately called 911. I would have called you then, hon, but everything happened so fast, and all we could think about was Laverne and getting her help. Anyway, this is the first chance I've had to call you."

Susan's mind was racing. "But she's okay? You're sure?"

"According to Dr. Willis, she's stable. He'll explain everything when you get here. You *are* coming, aren't you?"

"Yes, of course, I'm coming. But I can't leave until I find someone to come and wait here for Scott so he'll know where I am. He went into Austin to the circus and there's no way for me to get in touch with the person he's with. But as soon as I make those arrangements, I'll be there.''

"I'm in the waiting area outside critical care. It's on the third floor.''

As soon as they'd hung up, Susan called Amy, her friend and neighbor. Amy immediately said she'd be there, and five minutes later, she was. Five minutes after that, Susan was on her way to Tri-City General, the hospital that served the same three towns served by the community college.

It took her forty minutes to reach the hospital, find a parking place, and get to the third-floor critical-care waiting area. When she walked off the elevator, she immediately saw the group of women sitting together near the windows. Birdie, a big-boned woman in her seventies, stood, followed by Marian Schuler, a petite former schoolteacher in her mid-sixties, and Virginia Jacoby, Laverne's neighbor. They walked toward her.

Seeing them all there, with their worried faces and sympathetic eyes, caused the fear Susan had been holding back to break loose. Trembling and tearful, she let Birdie enfold her in her capable arms. The others fluttered around her, murmuring words of comfort and support.

When Susan once again had herself under control, Birdie said, "Go tell that woman who you are. She'll call Dr. Willis and tell him you're here and they'll let you go in to see Laverne.''

Susan belatedly noticed the volunteer who sat behind a registration desk. She walked over and identified herself. The woman picked up the phone and spoke into it softly. When she replaced the receiver, she inclined her head toward a set of double doors at the far end of the room.

"You can go in. The nurses' station is just inside, to the right. Tell them who you are and they'll take you to your mother-in-law."

Five minutes later, Susan was standing at the side of Laverne's bed. She blinked back tears, even though Laverne was sleeping and couldn't see them.

Please, God, she prayed. *Please don't take her. Scott and I need her. We love her. Please give us more time with her.*

Laverne looked smaller lying there. Smaller and so helpless. There was something about all those tubes and machines that brought home the fact that, in the end, most of us have to leave our fate in the hands of others.

Susan lightly touched Laverne's hand. *I love you, Mom. Please fight. Please don't leave us.*

"Mrs. Sheridan?"

Susan turned at the sound of the low voice to see Laverne's physician standing behind her. She hadn't heard his approach.

"Let's go out there," he said softly. "We can talk."

They walked back to the critical-care waiting area and he gave her a careful explanation of exactly what had happened to her mother-in-law. "Now, you know I'm not a cardiologist, but there is one on staff here, and he's the one who read her EKG and is overseeing her care. He'll talk to you, too, later tonight. He and I concur that the heart attack she suffered was a major one, but we've both seen patients pull through even worse attacks and go on to lead fairly healthy lives afterwards, especially if they follow the prescribed regime.''

"But you do think she'll pull through?''

He shrugged. "I hope she will. So far, things look promising. We've stabilized her and she's resting comfortably. The next twenty-four hours will tell the tale, though.''

They talked awhile longer, then the doctor said he was leaving for the night. "But Dr. Mullins will be here, and when he leaves, there will be another specialist on call. So there's no need to worry that your mother-in-law won't have good care. She'll be monitored carefully and they'll be called immediately if there's any change or any cause for concern. Plus I'll just be a phone call away.''

Susan thanked him warmly. She felt better for talking to him, even though she knew she wouldn't be able to relax completely until Laverne was totally out of the woods. She rejoined Laverne's friends and told them what Dr. Willis had said. "Thank you all for coming,'' she said when she was finished. "I really appreciate it.''

"I'll stay here with you tonight, Susan,'' Birdie said.

"Oh, Birdie, you don't have to do that.''

"I don't want you to be alone.''

"We're staying, too,'' the others echoed.

It took Susan some time to convince the three of them that she didn't want them to spend the night. But it wasn't until she said they'd be no good to her tomorrow if they didn't get any sleep that they finally acquiesced and said their goodbyes. She was relieved to see them go. Yes, it would have been nice to have company, especially Birdie's, but none of the women were exactly spring chickens, and she knew a sleepless night would take much more of a physical toll on them than it would on her.

Once they were gone she walked over to the courtesy phone and called home. Amy answered on the second ring. After giving her an update, Susan gave her the number of the waiting area and told her to have Keith call her when he and Scott returned.

"Don't tell Scott what happened," she cautioned. "Just say his grandmother is sick and I wanted to come and be with her."

"Oh, I wouldn't," Amy assured her. "Good luck, hon. Try not to worry. Everything's going to be all right."

They said goodbye. By now it was nearly ten o'clock. Susan walked over to the windows and looked out. To the east she could see the lights of Rainbow's End. All those people, she thought, going about their ordinary lives, some of them watching TV, some of them reading, some making love, some already in bed and asleep. And all of them blissfully unaware that in an instant their lives could change irrevocably, just as Laverne's had changed tonight.

Please, God, she prayed again. *Let her be all right.*

She stood there a long time. Then she sighed and walked to the closest chair and sat down to wait.

Keith thought Scott would fall asleep on the drive home, but he was too wired. Instead, the two of them rehashed the evening, talking about the things they'd liked best about the circus.

It was well after midnight when Keith pulled into Susan's driveway. The living-room lights were on, as was the outside light over the front door. He smiled. "Your mom's waiting for you."

But when the front door opened, it wasn't Susan standing there. It was a tall redhead Keith didn't recognize.

"Oh, hi, Mrs. Russell," Scott said. He frowned. "Where's Mom?"

"Hello, Scott," the woman said. Her brown eyes met Keith's. "Hi. I'm Amy Russell, Susan's neighbor."

"Keith Callahan," Keith said in confusion. What was going on?

Amy Russell turned her gaze to Scott. "Your grandmother is sick, and your mom wanted to go to the hospital to be with her."

"Gran?" Scott said. "What's wrong with her?"

"Nothing bad, honey," she said. "Your mom will tell you all about it tomorrow morning. In the meantime, you're to come and spend the night at my house, okay? Won't that be fun?" She reached in her pocket and pulled out a slip of paper. She handed it to Keith. "Susan wants you to call her."

Keith nodded. He could see by the expression in her eyes that she had tempered the truth for Scott's benefit. With a feeling of disquietude, he excused himself and headed for the phone in the kitchen.

"Yes," he said to the unfamiliar voice that answered the phone, "may I speak with Susan Sheridan, please?"

A few moments later, Susan said, "Keith?"

"Yes. What happened?"

"Scott can't hear you, can he?"

"No, I'm in the kitchen, and he's in the living room with your friend."

"Good."

Keith listened quietly as Susan told him about Paul's mother. When she'd finished, he said, "Are you there by yourself?"

"Yes."

"Where, exactly, are you?"

"Outside critical care, on the third floor."

He looked at his watch. It was twelve-thirty. "I'm coming. I'll be there in less than an hour."

She was silent, and for a few seconds, he thought she was going to tell him not to come. When she did speak, her voice sounded funny, and he knew she was on the verge of tears. "Thank you. Now can I please talk to Scott?"

When Scott finished talking to his mother, he came back into the living room. He looked subdued. "I hope my gran's gonna be all right."

"Oh, honey, I'm sure she is," Amy said quickly.

Keith gave him a reassuring smile. "She's going to be fine."

Scott sighed. "I guess I'll go get my stuff." Five minutes later he was back downstairs and ready to go.

"I'll talk to you tomorrow," Keith told Scott as they all walked outside together.

"Okay," Scott said, waving as he and Amy started across the lawn to her house. "Thanks for taking me to the circus."

Keith made it to the hospital in under thirty minutes. During the drive, he wondered if he was doing the right thing. Susan was vulnerable right now. Had he taken advantage of that vulnerability?

But when he got to the third-floor waiting area, he took one look at her and knew he hadn't made a mistake in coming. This wasn't the time to worry about the awkwardness of their situation or what might or might not happen between them in the future. Even if Susan never married him, Keith was her friend, and she needed a good friend right now.

He walked over to where she was seated. A moment later, she was in his arms. He held her for long minutes, trying to convey without words that no matter what, he would always be there for her when she needed him.

Whatever awkwardness they'd felt earlier in the evening disappeared, and when he released her, they sat next to each other and talked softly. When it was time for Laverne to have visitors again, Susan looked at him questioningly. "I won't be gone long. They'll only let me stay ten minutes, but if you want to go…"

"I'm not going anywhere." He squeezed her hand. "You go on. I'll be right here when you get back."

She nodded, and in her eyes he saw relief and something else. Something that reinforced his theory that she cared for him just as much as he cared for her.

As she walked toward the doors to the critical care unit, he watched her with a mixture of pride and love. I'll always be here for you, Susan. Almost as if she'd heard his silent promise, she turned. Their eyes met briefly before she opened the doors and disappeared inside.

Laverne was still asleep. Susan stood at her bedside and watched her for as long as the hospital personnel would allow her to. She felt stronger now, much more able to cope with whatever tomorrow would bring.

She knew that nothing had changed between her and Keith. They could never have the kind of relationship they both wanted, but tonight had shown her that he would always be her friend.

And somehow, she would have to make that be enough.

Chapter Fourteen

Susan knew she would never have gotten through the past few days if it hadn't been for Keith. He'd been a rock. He'd stayed at the hospital with her all night Saturday and all day Sunday. He'd only left after Dr. Mullin came out at nine o'clock Sunday night to tell them Laverne's condition had improved greatly, and he was confident she was going to make it. "She's awake now, and she wants to see you," he finished, smiling at Susan.

Susan trembled from relief and exhaustion. She had slept very little since she'd arrived the night before—mostly dosing in the chair—and the sleep hadn't been restful.

"Oh, thank God. Thank God." She wasn't sure she could have borne losing Laverne so soon after losing Paul. Smiling through eyes filmed with happy tears, she turned to Keith. "I really appreciate your staying with me, but why don't you go home now? I'm probably going to go myself after I see Laverne."

He squeezed her shoulder. "I'll wait until you come out."

And he had. Susan had gone in to see her mother-in-law who, although awake, was still terribly weak and tired very quickly. Susan only stayed about fifteen minutes before the attending nurse suggested that she leave. By the time Susan told Laverne she was going home and would be back in the morning, Laverne's eyes were already closed.

Keith had followed Susan home to make sure she got there okay, and on Monday, he'd shown up at the hospital on his lunch hour. Susan's heart warmed at the sight of him.

After first asking about Laverne, he said, "Can I do anything to help? I'm off at four."

Susan asked him if he would mind picking Scott up from Amy's house and bringing him to the hospital. "I was going to go get him, but if you wouldn't mind..."

"Consider it done," he said. He'd picked Scott up again on Tuesday, too.

Now it was Wednesday and Susan, at Laverne's urging, had gone into the office for a few hours. But Tom gently chided her and told her they could get along without her for a few more days. "You go on," he said. "I know you want to be at the hospital, and that's where you *should* be."

Giving him a grateful smile, she headed straight for the hospital, and when she arrived she had a pleasant surprise awaiting her. Laverne had been moved from critical care to a private room. Was, in fact, propped up in bed when Susan walked in. Several bouquets of flowers and a couple of plants lined the windowsill, and Laverne—although still hooked up to oxygen and an IV, as well as a heart monitor—was wearing the pretty pink bedjacket Susan had brought the day before.

"Mom! Oh, this is wonderful!" Susan exclaimed.

Her mother-in-law smiled. The smile was weak, and she still looked terribly pale, but it was clear she was definitely on the mend.

Susan bent over the bed and kissed Laverne's cheek. Her skin felt dry and papery. Love nearly overwhelmed Susan, and when she straightened, she knew Laverne could see the tears in her eyes.

Laverne smiled gently. "Don't cry, dear."

"They are happy tears."

"I know."

Susan pulled a chair up close and sat down. She reached for Laverne's hand. "I am so glad you're doing better. You scared me."

Laverne nodded. "I know. I was scared, too. I really thought I was going to die."

Susan's eyes filled with tears again. Darn, she thought, brushing them away. What's wrong with me? I'm supposed to be the strong one here. Lovingly, she squeezed Laverne's fingers. "Well, you're not. In fact, Dr. Mullin says you can live a long, long time if you're careful and follow his orders."

Laverne nodded again and sighed. "You know, when something like this happens, you really start to think."

"Yes," Susan agreed. "You realize what's important and what's not."

"Exactly," Laverne said. "I've been doing a lot of thinking the past couple of days, and there are some things I have to tell you."

"Mom," Susan said. "Whatever it is, it can wait."

"No, no, it can't."

Susan started to protest again, but Laverne cut her off, saying, "Susan, please let me talk. The first thing I wanted to tell you is, I love you. I think you know that, but maybe you don't know how much."

Susan swallowed. "I love you, too," she whispered.

"You made Paul so happy," Laverne continued. "You're a wonderful person, Susan. Giving and loving. You're such a good mother, and you were a wonderful wife to Paul. I appreciate everything you've ever done for him and for me. I've often thought that I couldn't love you more if you were my own daughter."

Susan was so touched, she couldn't speak.

Laverne sighed. "That was the easy part of what I needed to say."

Something about her tone and the expression in her eyes gave Susan a funny feeling.

"But with hard things, I've learned the best way is just to say them." Her gaze was loving as it rested on Susan's face. "I know you've been bewildered by the way I've acted toward Keith Callahan,'' Laverne continued slowly. ''By the way I've tried to keep you from seeing him.''

Susan could only stare at her mother-in-law. Of all the things Laverne could have said, this had been the farthest from Susan's mind.

''I suppose you've wondered why.''

Susan nodded slowly. ''Yes, I have.''

Laverne's fingers clasped Susan's hand more tightly. ''I acted that way because...because...I knew,'' she whispered.

''Knew?'' Susan said. ''Knew what?'' Her heart beat faster at the expression in Laverne's eyes. What was her mother-in-law talking about?

''The moment I saw Keith in your kitchen that first day, I knew he was Scott's father.''

Susan's heart nearly stopped. Her mouth fell open. She knew shock had drained her face of color.

''It's okay,'' Laverne said. ''I'm not accusing you. I just wanted you to know that I know, because I imagine you've been torturing yourself over this.''

Susan bit her bottom lip. All she could do was nod and stare at Laverne. Her mind reeled. Had Paul told Laverne he hadn't fathered her child when they got married? Had Laverne known about Scott all these years?

''Paul didn't tell me Scott wasn't his, if that's what you're thinking.''

Susan swallowed. ''Then I—I don't understand,'' she finally got out.

''You see, my dear, Paul was sterile.''

"I know that, b-but he said you *didn't* know about it."

"Did he?" Laverne sighed deeply. "I wondered. In fact, I wondered if *you* knew."

"But..." Susan stopped in confusion. "If you knew, what did you think when we got married and you found out I was pregnant?"

"I just thought that somehow, by some miracle, the doctors had been wrong."

"What made you change your mind? Did Paul say something?"

"Oh, no. Paul never said a word. Mind you, he never lied and said he'd fathered Scott or that he wasn't sterile as we'd been told. All he said was, Susan is pregnant, and the baby will be born in December. I suppose he thought if I wanted to know anything further, I would ask, and since I didn't, he didn't explain."

Susan could hardly take it all in. The secret was out, and Laverne didn't seem upset. The fact that Paul had lied to her when he told her Laverne didn't know about his sterility was something she would have to think about later. Right now the important thing was Laverne and what she knew and how she felt about it.

"When I saw Keith that day," Laverne said, "everything fell into place. And I got scared. So scared. All I could think was, now Susan will tell Keith that Scott is his son and then I'll lose Scott and probably her, too. I couldn't have borne it, Susan."

"Oh, Mom," Susan said, once again near tears.

"You'd *never* lose us. *I* was afraid if you knew I'd lose *you!*"

They both cried for a while after that, but the tears were good tears, happy tears, because each realized that the bonds they'd forged over the past ten years were as strong as any blood link could ever be.

"Keith doesn't know, does he?" Laverne said when their emotions were finally under control again.

"No."

"Doesn't even suspect?"

Susan shook her head. "We…we were only together one time. It…" She closed her eyes. This was so hard. But Laverne deserved an explanation. "It happened one night when Keith was in Austin visiting Paul. Paul and I weren't engaged or anything, but still, I knew it was wrong of us, and Keith knew it, too. In fact, he was so upset by what happened between us that he left Austin the next morning and soon after that, he left Rainbow's End."

"So he never knew you were pregnant."

"No."

"Why didn't you tell him?"

Susan sighed. "I—it's complicated. I—" She stopped. How could she tell Laverne that she hadn't wanted Keith that way? That she'd wanted him to love her, the way she loved him? Wouldn't Laverne hate her for marrying Paul when she felt that way about another man? "I just couldn't."

"Did Paul know the baby was Keith's?"

Susan shook her head. "No." She went on to explain how she'd broken up with Paul after the episode with Keith. How she and Paul had run into each other when she was five months pregnant. How shocked he'd been. And how the marriage proposal had come about.

By the time she'd finished telling Laverne everything, Laverne's eyes were filled with sadness.

"You must despise me now," Susan said.

"Oh, Susan, no. Please don't think that. I meant what I said before. You made Paul very happy. And you gave me a grandson."

Susan's eyes filled with tears again. Laverne was a remarkable woman. She'd always known it, but she'd never realized just how remarkable.

They were quiet for a few moments, then Laverne said, "I hated Keith for a while. I wanted to think of him as the villain, but deep down I knew he wasn't. He's a good man, Susan. And I think he deserves to know about Scott."

Susan knew what saying that must have cost Laverne. "You do? You think I should tell him?"

"Yes. It's obvious to me that he loves Scott already, and Scott loves him. I think he deserves to know the truth."

"But what about Scott?"

Laverne's face twisted. "Selfishly, I wish he didn't have to know, but I'm afraid Keith would want to tell him, and...well, we couldn't blame him if he did."

Susan bit her lip.

"M-maybe *you* want to tell him..."

"No," Susan said quickly, even though part of her did want Scott to know about Keith. "I'm afraid the knowledge would hurt Scott."

Their eyes met, and Susan's heart ached for the pain she saw in her mother-in-law's. "I'm not sure what the right thing is to do." She sighed deeply. "I know one thing, though. I'm not going to do anything right away. This whole situation is too serious to act without thinking it through carefully." She gave Laverne an encouraging smile. "And I don't want you to worry. We'll talk again before I take any action at all."

A tear slipped down Laverne's face. "Thank you," she whispered.

"You're the one who deserves thanks," Susan said.

Their emotional discussion had taken its toll on Laverne, for now she seemed completely exhausted and fell into a deep sleep. Susan sat by her bedside and watched her sleep, while her own mind whirled. She still couldn't take in everything. That Laverne knew about Keith and wasn't angry, that she even thought Susan should tell him the truth, was mind-boggling. Susan thought about how she'd agonized over Laverne, and now here she was, giving Susan carte blanche to do whatever she felt she should do.

Susan wanted to tell Keith. She wanted to tell him in the worst way. But even though the problem of Laverne was solved, there was a much bigger consideration with Scott. If she could be sure the truth was something he could handle, she would tell him in a heartbeat. But he had adored Paul. And even though he had a bad case of hero-worship where Keith was concerned, might that not change if he knew the truth? Might he not hate Keith? The truth could devastate him.

Could Susan take that chance?

Could she take her happiness at Scott's expense?

Keith stopped going to the hospital after Wednesday night when he discovered that Paul's mother had been moved into a private room. In fact, he didn't even see Susan on Wednesday, because once he found out about Laverne's changed condition and circumstances, he left without ever going to her floor. He knew Laverne would not want to see him. She'd made her feelings about him obvious, and the last thing he wanted to do was upset her, which would, in turn, upset Susan.

He did call Susan later, though. He got the answering machine and left a message saying that he was very glad Laverne was out of woods. He also said he'd be happy to do anything to help, all Susan had to do was call. He asked about Scott and finished by saying he hoped she'd keep him updated on Laverne's progress.

Later that night, lying in bed, he wondered how Scott was doing. The kid had been awfully worried about his grandmother. It would have been terrible if Laverne had died, especially so soon after Scott lost his dad. That would have left just him and his mother, for there were no other relatives.

Keith couldn't help comparing Scott's family to his own. He knew he was lucky. He might complain about his family's nosiness once in a while, but all in all, he sure was glad he had them.

Scott needed brothers and sisters. And he'd have them, if Keith could only persuade Susan to marry him. Even if they never had a child, Scott would still gain so much if they married. He'd have tons of cousins and aunts and uncles. And he'd have Keith's parents.

Keith could just see his mother and the way she'd fuss over Scott. She would take him to her heart the same way she took her natural grandchildren.

Keith smiled, thinking of it. After a while, no one in his family would even remember Scott wasn't his. Shoot, some people *already* thought Scott was his son. That really was funny, how Lorrie Carmichael had sworn Scott had the Callahan eyes.

I'd have known him anywhere. He looks just like you.

For some reason, after remembering her comments, Keith couldn't wipe them out of his mind, and it was hours before he fell asleep.

For the next two days, Lorrie's words continued to nag at Keith. Finally, on Friday afternoon, he decided he had to check something out. So after work, he stopped by his parents' house before heading home. He found his mother in the kitchen and a big pot of beans on the stove.

"Hey, Mom, what happened to those albums of us when we were kids?" he asked after giving her a hello kiss on the cheek.

"They're all stacked in boxes in the guest-room closet. Why?"

"I just wanted to look at them. You mind if I take a few of them home?"

"No. Of course not. Help yourself." She smiled and began stirring her beans.

Armed with half a dozen of the photo albums and a plastic container of beans that his mother had insisted he take, Keith headed home to his town house. After showering and changing into clean clothes, he sat down with a beer and starting looking through the albums. Before long, he found what he wanted.

He stared at the photos of himself when he was Scott's age. Lorrie Carmichael had been right. Except for the color of his hair and the smattering of freckles on his face, Scott looked *exactly* the way Keith had looked when he was ten. Same-shaped face, same body type, same stance, same features, same smile, and the same eyes.

Callahan eyes.

I would have known him anywhere.

And this must be your son. He looks exactly like you.

Those Callahan eyes...

Keith could hardly breathe. He closed the album. Swallowed. Stared off into space. Remembered something that had happened at the spaghetti dinner. The way Susan had stammered when she'd said Scott's birthday was December 20th.

His mind counted backwards. December to November. November to October.

March. Scott had been conceived sometime around the third week of March.

That was the year I went to Austin the third week of March.

He remembered how he'd suspected Paul and Susan weren't having sex. Paul had even hinted as much when he'd said Susan wouldn't move in with him. That she had high principles. He remembered how, from the very first meeting, he'd felt Susan didn't have the same feelings toward Paul as he had toward her.

And then there was *that night.* Keith hadn't used a condom because he hadn't planned to have sex with Susan.

His heart hammered.

Was it possible?

Was Scott his son?

Amazingly, Dr. Mullin released Laverne on Saturday, exactly one week after she'd suffered her heart attack. "She's doing so well, I see no reason why we need to keep her here. Of course," he added, "she's going to need help."

Susan worried about what to do. Should she bring Laverne to her house? But if she did, how would she care for her? She would have to quit her job. The thought made her feel sick, for as much as she loved Laverne and wanted to do whatever it took to help her get well, Susan did not want to quit her job. She loved it.

But her dilemma was solved quickly. Birdie Collier showed up at the hospital Saturday morning and announced to Susan that she and Laverne had discussed it and Laverne wanted to go home.

"But Mom," Susan said, "you're going to need help."

"I know that, and Birdie and her sister have agreed they'll stay with me until I'm strong enough to be on my own again."

"My sister Winona's a retired nurse," Birdie said. "Between us, we can handle anything that needs handling." She grinned at Laverne. "Including this stubborn woman here." Turning her smile Susan's way, she added in a softer voice, "Don't worry, Susan. We'll make sure she follows her instructions to the letter."

And so later that afternoon, Susan and Birdie between them managed to get Laverne settled at home. Then, leaving Scott with his grandmother, both of them under the watchful eyes of Birdie and Winona Collier, Susan went to the supermarket to buy groceries for Laverne and to the pharmacy to fill her prescriptions. By six o'clock Birdie had a tempting stew simmering on the stove, Winona was entertaining Scott with a game of checkers, and Laverne was resting in her favorite chair in front of a cozy fire in the living room.

For the first time in a week, Susan was able to relax completely. She pushed her problems out of her mind, and just enjoyed being there. She and Scott had supper with the three older women, then at eight, when Laverne's eyes were drooping, they kissed her goodbye and said they'd be back to check on her the next day.

That night, though, Susan's problems once more came to the fore, especially after Scott was asleep and she was alone in bed with nothing to do but think.

Keith, oh, Keith.

She had missed seeing him the past few days. She had missed talking to him, too. She had thought about calling him, but then she hadn't. What was the use? The more she saw him, the harder it was for her when he wasn't there, especially since she had decided she couldn't tell him about Scott. She just couldn't gamble with Scott's well-being that way, no matter how much it hurt.

She wished she could stop thinking about Keith, but her mind refused to cooperate. She wondered what he was doing now. Whether he was thinking of her the way she was thinking of him.

Sooner or later, he won't be, she thought sadly. He'll get tired of waiting for me to change my mind and gradually, he'll draw away from me. Then, one day, he'll meet someone else and fall in love with her. And that'll be the end.

The thought was devastating.

To all intents and purposes, Keith was already lost to her. And there wasn't one thing she could do about it.

All day Saturday Keith thought about what he should do. Should he confront Susan with his suspicions? Or should he bide his time, just wait and see what happened?

But after spending a more or less sleepless night, Keith knew he couldn't wait. He had to know the truth. At nine o'clock, fortified by three cups of coffee, he called Susan's house. She answered on the second ring.

"Oh, hi, Keith."

"Hi. How's Paul's mother doing?"

"She's doing great. I—I meant to call you yesterday, then time sort of got away from me. Laverne's at home now. We took her home yesterday."

"That's terrific."

There was an awkward silence, then he said, "Uh, listen, Susan, there's something I have to talk to you about."

"Oh. Okay." There was a cautious note to her voice that hadn't been there before.

"Is Scott home?"

"No, he's gone to Sunday School."

"Do you mind if I come over, then?"

"Well, um, after he gets home we're supposed to go over to Laverne's."

"This won't take long."

"I—"

"I'll see you in about fifteen minutes." He hung up before she could say a flat-out *no*.

Thirteen minutes later he rang her doorbell.

She opened the door so quickly, Keith wondered if she'd been waiting in the entryway. She looked tired, he thought.

She gave him a welcoming smile, although her eyes were wary. "I have coffee made. Would you like some?"

He shook his head. "I've had too much already this morning." Now that he was here, he wondered if he was crazy to think what he was thinking.

She frowned. "What's wrong, Keith?"

"Look, you might think I'm nuts, but something happened while Scott and I were at the circus, and ever since I've been thinking about it."

"What?" Now she looked alarmed.

"It...what happened doesn't really matter. It's just that because of what happened, I've come to believe something that has thrown me a real curve."

Suddenly still, she stared at him. The silence throbbed between them.

He took a deep breath. "I think Scott is my son."

Chapter Fifteen

Susan knew all the color had drained from her face. She opened her mouth, but no words came out.

His eyes were like blue lasers as they bored into hers. "Is it true?" he demanded. "*Is* he my son?"

She began to tremble. The time for lies was past. "Yes." The word came out in a hoarse whisper.

Keith stared at her. He could see the tears in her eyes, but he felt no sympathy for her. Two emotions warred within him—elation and anger. The elation was because his suspicion was correct: he was the father of the wonderful kid he'd wished was his so many times. The fury was caused by a lot of things: the fact that Susan had kept the knowledge from him. The fact that he'd missed out on so many years of Scott's life. But he was mostly furious with himself, because if he hadn't run off all those years ago, if he'd stayed and faced the music like a man, the entire scenario would have been completely different.

"I'm sorry, Keith," she said brokenly. The tears spilled over, running down her face.

In the face of her distress, his anger disappeared. Her eyes beseeched him to understand. Compassion and love for her crowded out all the lesser emotions.

"Susan..." He reached for her.

All the worry and anxiety of the past week, added to the shock of the past few minutes, were too much for Susan. She completely lost it when she felt his arms go around her. He held her until she'd cried herself out, then gently, he led her into the living room. He sat on the couch and pulled her down next to him.

"Tell me everything," he said, "from the beginning."

And so she did. It was hard at first, but it got easier. She told him how she'd broken up with Paul after Keith left Austin that night so long ago. "I'd always known I didn't love Paul the way I should, and what happened between us, well, that just reinforced what I knew I had to do."

He didn't comment, just nodded his understanding, so she continued.

She told him how she had realized she was pregnant and how she'd agonized over whether to get in touch with him and tell him. "I actually picked up the phone once, but...but I chickened out."

"Hell, I don't blame you," he said bitterly. "You

probably thought I was a complete loser after the way I ran out on you.''

''That wasn't the reason. I...'' Oh, God, this was so hard, but now that the truth about Scott's parentage was out, Susan wanted Keith to know everything. ''I never thought of you that way. The trouble was, I'd...I'd fallen in love with you. And I was afraid, once you knew about the pregnancy, you'd offer to marry me even though you didn't love me. I—I couldn't have stood that. I didn't want you that way.''

''Oh, Susan, I—''

''No,'' she said. ''Don't say anything. Not yet. Let me finish.''

She told him how she'd run into Paul when she was five months pregnant. How shocked he was. How they'd talked and how she'd learned that Keith had gone away. She explained how Paul had proposed to her and how he'd told her he was sterile.

''He made me think that I would be doing something wonderful for him, too,'' she said sadly. ''At first, when I found out he'd lied to me and that his mother knew about his sterility all the time, I was angry. But now I realize he told me that to make it easy for me to say yes.'' Her voice broke again as she added, ''He was a wonderful man.''

''Yes,'' Keith said. A look of pain was etched across his face. ''Do you think he suspected I was Scott's father?''

''No.''

''And he never asked you again?''

''No.''

They sat quietly for a few moments, each lost in their own thoughts. Then Susan said, "After you came back to Rainbow's End, I wanted to tell you the truth so many times. But I just didn't know how I could."

She explained her reasoning, and he shook his head in agreement when she told him about Laverne. "I just couldn't hurt her like that. I thought she'd be devastated to find out Scott wasn't really her grandson." Then she went on to tell him that Laverne guessed the truth that first day she'd seen Keith after his return home.

"So that's it. No wonder she was so hostile to me."

"Yes, she said she was terribly afraid she'd lose Scott. And me."

For the next ten minutes Susan relayed everything she and Laverne had talked about, especially how Laverne had urged her to tell Keith the truth.

"So she's not upset?" Keith said.

"Well, she is, but I think she knows now that no matter what happens, she won't lose me *or* Scott. I will always consider her my family, and Scott will always think of her as his grandmother."

Keith frowned and looked away.

"Keith?" Susan said softly. "What are you thinking?"

He sighed deeply and turned his gaze back to hers. "I'm thinking how much I love you. You and Scott." He stroked her cheek, looking deeply into her eyes. Then he kissed her—a long, cleansing kiss that washed away all the pain of the past weeks. "Susan," he whispered. "Do you love me, too?"

Her heart was so full. "I've always loved you."

He smiled crookedly. "So you'll marry me, then?"

"I—I want to, but—"

"But what?"

"You...I suppose you will want to tell Scott the truth."

His arms tightened around her. "I thought I did, but now I don't know. Is it right to take Paul away from him?" The next words were the hardest he'd ever had to say, but suddenly he knew they were what should be said. "Maybe we shouldn't tell him."

"Oh, Keith." Her voice broke, and fresh tears pooled in her eyes. "I was afraid to suggest it, but now that you have, I think not telling him is the right thing to do." She brushed away the tears, but her beautiful eyes were still filled with sorrow. "I'm so sorry. I wish things could be different."

"Yes, I do, too. But Scott's welfare is the most important consideration here. It'll be adjustment enough having a stepfather." He was struck by a new thought. What if Scott wasn't happy about him and Susan getting married?

"Don't worry," she said, reading his mind. "He'll be happy about us. I'm sure of it."

Susan hoped she was right, because if, for some reason, Scott *wasn't* happy about Keith becoming a part of their family, she didn't know what she'd do.

She couldn't bear to give Keith up again. Not now. Not after everything they'd been through. Not when she'd finally found him again.

She was so happy. She couldn't believe how happy she was. All afternoon at Laverne's, she wished she could tell her mother-in-law about the morning's developments, but she couldn't—not until she and Keith had had a chance to talk to Scott alone. They had considered doing it this morning, but she was afraid if Scott was upset, he'd upset Laverne. So she and Keith had decided to wait until tonight. Then, if all went well, the two of them would go to talk to Laverne together tomorrow.

Now she and Scott were on their way home, where Keith would be waiting. Her heart lifted in happiness, even as she worried about Scott's reaction to their news. She thought he would be thrilled, but there was always a chance he wouldn't be. Well, she'd soon know.

"Mom, Keith's here!" Scott said as they pulled into the driveway. Keith's truck was parked in front of the house.

"Yes," Susan said. "I knew he was coming."

"Why didn't you *tell* me?"

Before Susan could answer, Scott had yanked open the passenger door. He was already racing across the lawn to meet Keith, who stood on the front walk waiting for him. Susan followed more slowly. Their eyes met, and a silent exchange of love was delivered. He smiled, and she smiled back.

"Hi," he said when she reached them.

"Hi."

"You wanna shoot some baskets?" Scott said excitedly.

"Maybe later," Keith said. "First your mom and I have something we want to talk to you about."

"Oh." Scott looked at Susan. "Okay."

The three of them went into the house and Keith, with a questioning glance at Susan, said, "Want to go into the living room?"

She nodded, suddenly very nervous. What happened in the next few minutes would determine their entire future. Susan sat on the couch, and Scott sat next to her. Keith sat across from them in a leather chair.

"Scott," she began, "the reason Keith and I wanted to talk to you together is we have something important to tell you." She looked at Keith. The ball's in your court, she told him silently.

"I love your mom, Scott," Keith said, "and I've asked her to marry me."

Scott looked stunned. He looked at Susan. "Are you gonna, Mom?"

"I want to," Susan said, "but I wanted to be sure you were okay with it." She held her breath. *Please be happy about this, Scott.*

"Does…" Scott looked at Keith. "Does this mean you'd be my dad?"

It hurt Susan to see the flicker of pain that Keith quickly masked.

"I could never take the place of your dad," he said, "but I'd be honored to be your stepfather."

At that moment, Susan loved Keith more than she'd ever loved him before.

For a long moment, Scott said nothing. Susan was afraid to look at Keith. She was almost afraid to breathe. And then, in one wonderful instant that she knew she would remember forever, his face lit up with a huge smile.

"Cool," he said. He looked from Susan to Keith and back to Susan again. "I think Dad would really be happy about this."

Susan could barely talk over the lump in her throat. Her eyes met Keith's. In them, she saw everything she was feeling. Happiness, love, and most of all, thankfulness. They were finally going to be a family. "Yes," she said, "Yes, I do, too."

Two months later

From the pages of the *Rainbow's End Register:*

Susan Carroll Sheridan and Keith Torrance Callahan were married yesterday evening in a candlelight ceremony at Holy Family Parish. The date had special significance for the couple, because it was the tenth birthday of Susan's son, Scott.

The bride looked radiant in an off-white satin designer gown and floral headpiece. She carried a bouquet of ruby-red roses and stephanotis. The groom looked handsome in a black tuxedo with red cummerbund and red bow tie. The church was decorated with white poinsettias, and white lights shone on all the garlands and Christmas trees.

The wedding party consisted of Jan Callahan, in red velvet, who was her new sister-in-law's matron of honor and Rory Callahan, brother of the groom, who was the best man. Briana Callahan, who wore a charming dress of dark green velvet and a matching headband, and Scott Sheridan, wearing a tux that matched his new stepfather's, were junior attendants.

In a touching and unusual moment, Mrs. Laverne Sheridan, widow of prominent Rainbow's End attorney Reginald Sheridan, and grandmother to Scott, gave away the bride.

A reception at the Rainbow's End Inn immediately followed the ceremony. The newlyweds, after a honeymoon in Italy, will live in Rainbow's End.

"Happy?"

Susan snuggled closer to her new husband. She sighed. "So happy it scares me."

They were spending their wedding night in Austin. Tomorrow morning they would begin their long trip to Italy, flying first to Houston, then to Paris, then to Venice, where they had reservations at a luxury hotel on the Grand Canal. But right now they were in the back seat of the limousine Keith had hired, on their way to their hotel.

"Not worried about Scott, are you?"

"No. He's thrilled to be staying with Patrick and Jan while we're gone." She chuckled. "Briana's thrilled, too."

"Yeah," Keith agreed, laughing. "I think it's

love. And speaking of love..." He tipped her face up and covered her mouth with his.

Heedless of the driver, Susan lost herself in the kiss. They were both breathing hard when they finally came up for air.

"I want you so much," he whispered into her ear.

"Me, too," she whispered back.

"When I get you in that hotel..." He brushed his hand over her breast, and her body responded immediately.

He smiled, moving his thumb back and forth across the fabric until she thought she would die of pleasure and need.

It had been a mutual decision to wait until they were married before having sex. They had both felt they wanted to start this second phase of their relationship the right way. But it had been harder than she'd imagined it would be to wait. Finally, though, the wait was nearly over.

A half hour later, they pulled up outside their hotel. It seemed to take forever for the bellman to load their luggage on the cart, for Keith to get them registered and get their room key, for their luggage to be transferred to their room, for Keith to tip the bellman, and for him to finally leave them alone.

As soon as the door shut behind him, Keith reached for her. But Susan gently resisted. "Let's change our clothes first, okay?" She was afraid that if they started kissing now she wouldn't ever get to put on the beautiful lavender satin gown trimmed in lace that Amy had given her.

"You're a hard woman," Keith grumbled.

"Just be ready when I come out." She blew him a kiss and, grabbing her overnight bag, headed for the bathroom.

It only took her ten minutes to change from her wedding finery to the gown and another five minutes to brush her teeth and hair and freshen her makeup and perfume.

She looked at herself in the mirror before going out to join Keith. She would do, she thought, smoothing the gown over her body. Taking a deep breath, she turned and opened the door.

Keith, clad only in low-riding black silk pajama bottoms, sat on the side of the turned-down bed. He had turned off all the lamps except the one at the bedside and opened the drapes. The lights of the city twinkled in the distance. He looked up as she walked out, and she could see by the widening of his eyes and the quickening of his breath that he approved. Suddenly shy, she dropped her gaze.

He got up and walked toward her.

"Susan." His voice sounded rough.

She looked up. Swallowed.

"You're not afraid, are you?" he murmured.

"I could never be afraid of you."

His eyes darkened. He put his hands on her shoulders, running them slowly down her arms, then back up again.

Susan shivered.

Leaning forward, he kissed her softly. Then, in one smooth motion, he scooped her up in his arms and carried her to the bed. For a long moment, he looked down at her. Her heart thumped crazily.

"You're so beautiful," he whispered. Then, smiling, he pulled at the drawstring waist of his pajamas. A second after that, he'd turned off the bedside lamp and gotten into bed beside her. Moonlight spilled into the room, gilding his body.

Susan touched his chest. "You're beautiful, too."

And then she was in his arms, and he was kissing her and touching her as she'd dreamed of being kissed and touched. She met his passion with an equal fire, and soon they could wait no longer. She cried out when they were finally united, and her heart filled with a joy so blinding, she was certain she must surely die of it.

Later, when they were lying together spoon-fashion, she knew that no matter how long she lived or how many times they made love, she would never forget this night.

I am finally home.

From the pages of the *Rainbow's End Register:*

A gala pre-Christmas party on Friday night marked the first anniversary of Keith and Susan Callahan, a popular young couple in Rainbow's End. About fifty of their friends and family were present to wish them well and congratulate them on the news that they are expecting their first child—a girl—in early June.

Susan, who was married to Paul Sheridan until the accident that claimed his life, has a son, Scott, who celebrated his eleventh birthday the night of the party. When asked how he felt about having a little sister, he grinned and said, "Cool."

* * * * *

Watch for sassy, independent Sheila Callahan to finally meet her match in the next installment of CALLAHANS & KIN—FALLING FOR AN OLDER MAN—coming in February, from Silhouette Special Edition....

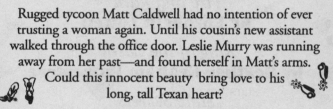

Start celebrating Silhouette's 20th anniversary
with these 4 special titles by
New York Times bestselling authors

Fire and Rain
by Elizabeth Lowell

King of the Castle
by Heather Graham Pozzessere

State Secrets
by Linda Lael Miller

Paint Me Rainbows
by Fern Michaels

On sale in December 1999

Plus, a special free book offer inside each title!

Available at your favorite retail outlet

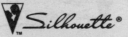

Visit us at www.romance.net   PSNYT

PAMELA TOTH
DIANA WHITNEY
ALLISON LEIGH
LAURIE PAIGE
bring you four heartwarming stories
in the brand-new series

So Many Babies

At the Buttonwood Baby Clinic,
babies and romance abound!

♥♥♥♥♥♥♥♥♥

On sale January 2000: **THE BABY LEGACY**
by Pamela Toth

On sale February 2000: **WHO'S THAT BABY?**
by Diana Whitney

On sale March 2000: **MILLIONAIRE'S INSTANT BABY**
by Allison Leigh

On sale April 2000: **MAKE WAY FOR BABIES!**
by Laurie Paige

Only from Silhouette SPECIAL EDITION
Available at your favorite retail outlet.

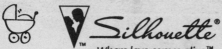

Silhouette®
Where love comes alive™

Visit us at www.romance.net

SSESMB

Don't miss Silhouette's newest cross-line promotion,

Four royal sisters find their own Prince Charmings as they embark on separate journeys to find their missing brother, the Crown Prince!

The search begins
in October 1999 and
continues through February 2000:

On sale October 1999: **A ROYAL BABY ON THE WAY**
by award-winning author **Susan Mallery** (Special Edition)

On sale November 1999: **UNDERCOVER PRINCESS**
by bestselling author **Suzanne Brockmann** (Intimate Moments)

On sale December 1999: **THE PRINCESS'S WHITE KNIGHT**
by popular author **Carla Cassidy** (Romance)

On sale January 2000: **THE PREGNANT PRINCESS**
by rising star **Anne Marie Winston** (Desire)

On sale February 2000: **MAN...MERCENARY...MONARCH**
by top-notch talent **Joan Elliott Pickart** (Special Edition)

ROYALLY WED
Only in—
SILHOUETTE BOOKS

Available at your favorite retail outlet.

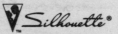

Visit us at www.romance.net

SSERW

Return to Whitehorn

Look for these bold new stories set in beloved Whitehorn, Montana!

CINDERELLA'S BIG SKY GROOM by Christine Rimmer
On sale October 1999 (Special Edition #1280)
A prim schoolteacher pretends an engagement
to the town's most confirmed bachelor!

A MONTANA MAVERICKS CHRISTMAS
On sale November 1999 (Special Edition #1286)
A two-in-one volume containing
two brand-new stories:

"Married in Whitehorn" by Susan Mallery
and
"Born in Whitehorn" by Karen Hughes

A FAMILY HOMECOMING by Laurie Paige
On sale December 1999 (Special Edition #1292)
A father returns home to guard his wife and child—
and finds his heart once more.

*Don't miss these books, only from
Silhouette Special Edition.*

Look for the next **MONTANA MAVERICKS** tale, by
Jackie Merritt, on sale in Special Edition May 2000.
And get ready for
MONTANA MAVERICKS: Wed in Whitehorn,
a new twelve-book series coming from Silhouette Books
on sale June 2000!

Available at your favorite retail outlet.